"They never send for me until the project starts falling apart, but I guess that's what sons-of-bitches are for."

—J.G.

THE
JUDAH LION
CONTRACT

Philip Atlee

A FAWCETT GOLD MEDAL BOOK

Fawcett Publications, Inc., Greenwich, Conn.

THE JUDAH LION CONTRACT

Copyright © 1972 by Fawcett Publications, Inc.

Printed in the United States of America
September 1972

IT is not every summer afternoon that a man can take his ease drinking honey wine and watching the Emperor's horses being stabled. On my private terrace in the Ghion Hotel, in the heart of Addis Ababa, I was sipping *tej* and watching the white-jodhpured *syces* of Haile Selassie curry his twenty private mounts and lead them into their stalls. The imperial stables were below the gardens of the hotel, and around them the Negus' capital spread across the high African plateau, framed by the blue ramparts of the Entoto Hills.

The Ethiopian metropolis was booming toward a million people, at nearly two miles above sea level. Tall buildings clustered across the valley; skeletal towers held huge cranes as they mounted. Many of the wide boulevards were still bordered by rows of small mud huts, but they were interspersed with modern apartment buildings and new government construction. The fabled Land of Sheba was cracking its primitive chrysalis, being propelled into the jet age.

I appreciated all this, and reflected that the source of the Blue Nile was not far north of where I sat. But there is a price for everything, and I was not a tourist. Putting down my jug of *tej*, I walked back into the suite. Through the sitting room and into the master bedroom beyond, to check on my charge.

His name was Dr. Claude Kalinga, O.B.E., with an Honours from Oxford in African Antiquities and a doctorate from the London School of Economics. He was an affable, urbane little man, extremely black, and until eighteen months ago had been President of the Republic of Marundi, a landlocked fiefdom in East Central Africa. His deposition had been abrupt, violent, and well-deserved; he had hard over the border by night, closely pursued by

5

Colonel Pangolin, his Defense Minister, the entire Marundian Army, and all citizens mobile enough to join the chase.

Now, as he had been doing since I had met him in Durban, he was working on his journal and composing philippics to bootleg back into his impoverished little land. He smiled cheerfully at me over the polished desk; the basalt head was impressive. Pince-nez glasses gave him a look of dignity, and his state of habitual constipation lent him a look of concern, although I could never understand how a man who drank as much as Dr. Kalinga could stay corked up.

Reassured, knowing there was a guard posted on the corridor doors, I returned to the terrace. All the Emperor's steeds had been stalled; their delicate Arabian heads were framed in the open, upper half-doors. I had another drink of *tej* and glanced through the *Ethiopian Herald*. A dispatch from Accra (Reuters) stated that a 24-year-old unemployed Ghanaian who had posed as an astronaut had been given a year in prison.

He had entered a village and introduced himself as a health officer, come to vaccinate the people against cholera. While setting up, he informed the village elders that he was the only Ghanaian to accompany the American astronauts into space. And described those remote reaches as "all golden sand with a mighty black rock, and footsteps, probably those of Jesus Christ . . ."

More to the point was a letter from an irate subscriber in Massawa, an Ethiopian port. Signing himself Able Seaman Abraham Debas, he wrote that "the city buses in Massawa don't only transport people, but also a good number of stinking fish. Because the seats are already overloaded by the stinking fish, passengers overload until at last a man sits on another man. This is especially unbearable for weak women . . ." Debas concluded by enquiring sternly who was responsible for this.

I didn't know, but I hoped that he was never forced into a New York subway, where the fish were just as strong and the women not so weak.

My revery was interrupted by a silent, white-clad servant who enquired if I wanted tea. Startled, I glanced at his dark, clean-cut features and asked him to wait a minute. I crossed to the far bedroom again, found it empty, and heard a great shouting begin below the suite windows. Running back to the terrace, nearly bowling the room-boy over, I saw pandemonium swirling in the paddock below.

Taxi drivers in the rank on the curving drive were shouting and *syces* were screaming in Amharic and running down the riding path. Ghion Hotel guests came hurrying out of the lounges, followed by servants, and all of them were staring at the palomino stallion being stampeded down the path between towering eucalyptus trees.

The small rider was crouched in flawless point-to-point style and wore a bowler hat jammed down on his conical black head. Even from the butt-end view I could recognize the ex-Excellency of Marundi, Dr. Kalinga. Silky white mane and tail rippling, the imperial stallion was booted around the turn. I stood motionless on the terrace, listening until the drumming hoofbeats had faded, knowing I was in deep trouble.

There was nothing to do, however, so that's what I did. Ordered another mug of *tej* and sat waiting. An hour passed, and twilight darkened beyond the terrace. Familiar neon symbols bloomed on the towers, and mingled among them were delicate scarlet traceries in Amharic. I heard the elevators at the end of the hall whine up, and a party of soldiers, heavy-footed, opened the suite door without ceremony.

A tall young officer in a British-type garrison cap entered first and enquired brusquely where Dr. Kalinga's quarters were. I nodded toward the master bedroom, and Dr. Kalinga was hustled past me and into his room. The door closed with finality. Claude had been minus his bowler hat, looked disheveled, and his stylish Savile Row suit had been ripped.

The young Ethiopian officer spoke to the other men in his squad, and they went out into the hall. Putting the garrison cap under one elbow, the officer asked my permission to sit down. I nodded, and asked if he would have a drink. A Scotch? Yes. The room boy was at my elbow, and I ordered two double Scotches, with ice and soda.

I did not say anything until the drinks came. The young officer was angry, with justification, and I had no idea what had happened. He had a dark Nilotic head and the air of unconscious arrogance most upper-class Ethiopians seem to inherit. When I lifted my drink, he responded readily and asked why I was escorting such an obvious lunatic as deposed President Kalinga around?

"A fair question, Colonel. I was ordered to."

"You are a military man?"

"No, but I was. The U.S. Marines."

"Oh?" The dark eyes flickered. "A brave corps, certainly; we study them in our War College. Possibly they lose too many men through frontal assault, when there are other ways?"

"That theory has been advanced," I agreed. "But I was a field-grade officer, and we did not debate general tactics."

He nodded. "Understood. And I am not yet a colonel, although I deserve to be after this chase. Do you know what this cretin from Marundi did?"

"No."

"He approached the head *syce*, at the stables below, and demanded that the Emperor's favorite stallion be saddled. Well, these stable people are always awed by European clothes and the accent, so the horse was prepared. Kalinga then vaulted aboard, lashed the animal past a main traffic intersection, and broke a red light in the process. Raced like a madman past the Filowha Baths, the Jubilee Palace, and along Menelik Avenue to the Hilton Hotel entrance.

"There he bowled the doorman aside, charged across a flowered verge, and lashed the horse down the outside steps to the swimming pool level. Batting at the stallion's flanks with his hat, he thrice circumnavigated the pool, knocking over beach umbrellas and forcing tourist bathers into panic flight."

The indignant young officer sipped his drink and shook his head at these breaches of decorum.

"An outrage," I agreed. "Presumably, he was drunk. I have only known him three days, but during that period he has always been loaded or aspiring to that condition."

The officer snorted. "Good enough, perhaps, in his land. In Ethiopia, we do not tolerate such things. For one thing, the horses are not accustomed; the Emperor is old and they are not much ridden. And after he had terrorized everyone, this fellow had the temerity to ride into the pool bar and demand a drink, still sitting on the horse!"

"Improper," I admitted. And when he continued to brood, "Shocking conduct."

Partially placated, the young officer thanked me for the drink and stood up. Replacing the garrison cap precisely, he said that he now had to report to the Palace. Dr. Kalinga was under room arrest, and unfortunately, so was I. We could order anything we wanted except more drink for the Doctor, but neither could leave the suite. Guards would be at all doors. I said I understood, we shook hands, and he left.

When I knocked on the door to Kalinga's bedroom, he shouted *"entrez-vous!"* He was stretched out on the bed naked, a dusky, overaged Pan, and waggled lumpish toes at me. But I wasn't watching him.

A tall, unsmiling black girl was standing beside his bed. She wore the white nylon uniform of a nurse, and had a white silk *shamma* thrown around her shoulders. *Bold!* I thought instantly, *prouder than God on one of His good days*. . . . No makeup that I could detect in that light, but she was high-breasted and her legs were long. One of those women who seem always to be bursting of their clothes, no matter how conventionally they are dressed. Her features were Hamitic, straight nose and chiseled mouth.

"My companion," explained Dr. Kalinga, and I wondered how he could have set up such a deal while careering around on a stolen horse. "After my ride, I felt . . . palpitations. So I engaged Miss Lalibela." He lurched toward the bed-table and poured himself a big drink of honey-mead. Offered her one, and she refused without changing her expression or taking her eyes off me. Kalinga winked. "Cost of medical care to be borne by the U.S.A., isn't that true?"

"I suppose so, Clyde," I said slowly. "At least until I am given different instructions. But you've made this Ethiopian Government angry, and they may give us the bum's rush. Even deportation."

"Pouf!" Kalinga poured another big drink. Downed it and tried to fondle the dark girl's breasts. She pushed his hands aside without anger. "And don't call me Clyde!" shouted the deposed Marundian President. "It is not my name. If I give you permission to address me with familiarity you may call me Claude."

"Sorry, kid," I said wearily. "To me, you will always be Clyde. It is a type, not a name."

Going into the bathroom off my own bedroom, I switched on the light and studied myself in the mirror. I think no man is ever completely sure of who he is, or what he has become. And often there is little help in the mirror.

What I could see was a square-headed malcontent of obvious Irish ancestry. Enough hair, sun-bleached so blond that the gray hardly showed; a regular visage with scarred eyebrows and an accidental rhinoplasty. . . . Some would think I had been perhaps a good, retired light-heavy who never made the Garden, but had money enough for regular massages.

Trim. You stay that way when strangers keep trying to kill you; it is a great aid to concentration. And if not quite the image of a retired polo player, I was still lean enough to look like a crooked vice-squad cop caught early and busted.

These conclusions would have been valid enough in Cleveland or San Francisco, but what do you do with them in Ethiopia? Shaking my head, I walked back into the sitting room of the suite. After a while, a real Ethiopian colonel came, flanked by four smartly turned-out rankers, to tell me that my presence was required immediately at the Jubilee Palace of Emperor Haile Selassie.

$\mathbf{T}$ HE black Mercedes sedan rolled past stiffened sentries and stone lions at the palace gates. The Emperor's pennons, flying from the fenders, were saluted; the car swept around the floodlit drive and stopped before the wide steps. The colonel escorted me to a set of inner guards and I was turned over to another officer, who asked my pardon and frisked me expertly.

He took me down an echoing corridor to the right, past scores of high, carved doors, to the office of one of the Emperor's private secretaries. This dignitary bowed from behind his desk, gave me his name, which I did not catch, and motioned for me to be seated. He was a small, intense man with high cheekbones, and could not have been more than thirty, although his neat Van Dyke beard was snowy at the tip.

He offered me tea, coffee, or a drink, but I refused. I knew I was probably violating protocol, but I don't work the protocol league. Leaning back, the slender secretary steepled his almost-feminine fingers under his showy beard and began to talk with precision.

"An unfortunate occurrence, personally distressing to His Imperial Majesty. He would ordinarily dismiss what happened as a drunken prank, below his notice. The fact remains, however, that His Majesty's favorite mount was involved in the peccadillo and this has already become local gossip. That alone would make us view it with distaste.

"Unfortunately, greater damage was done. Tomorrow a meeting of the Organization of African Unity states will convene here in Addis. Several delegations have already flown in; ministers from Gabon, Senegal, Mali, Niger, and Mauritania were at the Hilton poolside, or in the pool bar with their families, when drunken Dr. Kalinga came bursting in on The Negus' horse."

He smiled a wintry smile.

"What I suppose you Americans would call an *opéra bouffé* version of Paul Revere—"

"The fault is mine," I said. "He was placed in my care and outwitted me. I still don't know what happened to the guard on his bedroom door." This last was a subtle dilution of my *mea culpa;* the guard had been an Ethiopian security officer. The dandified little official did not miss the point; his wintry smile defrosted a trifle.

Watching him, I thought that the Emperor was well served. The secretary was precise and logical; before he started to speak, he knew where he would end. Not many people do that.

"When the proposal was made to us, several weeks ago and *sub rosa,* that we should afford a temporary sanctuary for Dr. Kalinga, we agreed with the understanding that his presence here be anonymous. This because we knew that General Pangolin's offer of a million shillings to anyone who would return him to Marundi alive would create great pressure. And if he did get seized and returned, he would receive a show trial for alleged excesses and barbarities while in office, matters which we are not competent to judge.

"The other element of General Pangolin's offer we thought demeaning to all black African states, no matter what Dr. Kalinga may have done. To announce that one East African pound would be paid for his return dead was to subject us all to ridicule in the chancelleries of the world. His Imperial Highness had known Dr. Kalinga slightly in London and other places, when he was a more moderate man. At that time, a man of considerable education, dignity, and tribal influence . . ."

The secretary leaned forward and I knew the hammer was about to fall.

"Now, however, his prank has obliterated these considerations. Tomorrow, General Pangolin will lead the Marundian Delegation when the OAU convenes, and his anger over this incident can be imagined. We have not been informed yet whether any of the guests at the Hilton recognized the horse's rider, but I should think some of them must have. If General Pangolin finds out, he will make every attempt to capture or kill Dr. Kalinga.

"And unfortunately, sir, murderers are as easy to hire in Ethiopia as they are in Chicago. Here we call them *shiftas,* and they come much cheaper."

The young secretary stood up, and I arose with him.

"Within the next two hours, you and Dr. Kalinga will vacate the Ghion Hotel suite. You will be furnished a Toyota Land-Cruiser with a military driver-guide, and one corporal. You will proceed out of Addis Ababa without delay, south, not stopping for at least twenty-four hours. All army-financial checkpoints have been instructed not to delay you. On the other hand, neither they nor your driver or corporal will protect you."

I nodded. It was a better break than I had expected. At the airport, we would have been sitting ducks.

"I am supposed to guard the man until I deliver him to a certain place on a certain day. Am I to be furnished any weapons with which to do this?"

"Yes. In the Land Cruiser there will be two carbines and two M-16 rifles, with extra ammunition for both. I hope you can keep Dr. Kalinga sober enough to use them. Our men will escort you to the southern border; from there you have access to the Sudanese, Kenyan, or Ugandan borders."

"Near enough," I said. "There is another matter, perhaps a minor one. After Dr. Kalinga was returned to the hotel, an attractive young lady turned up. He claims to have hired her as a nurse, but she appears to have other outstanding capabilities. Do I pay her off, and dismiss her?"

"No," said the Emperor's secretary patiently. "Kalinga

is lying. Her name is Maryam Lalibela. She *is* a nurse, and I sent her. Since you have to smuggle a drunken politician of fringe importance out of our kingdom, we want it done as quietly as possible. I thought she might be helpful."

He moved some papers on his desk, not thinking about them at all.

"I should warn you that Miss Lalibela is a Danakil, from the fiercest desert in our Eritrean coastal region. She has been engaged not only as a nurse for Kalinga, and a watchdog for me, but as his *damoz* consort. That is, a wife contracted for a short time. But if that fool abuses her, she will kill him before General Pangolin can do so."

It took me a few seconds to grasp the essence of Miss Lalibela's attachment to our group. I told the secretary we would vacate the Ghion suite as soon as possible, and bowed to him. He returned the bow like a small Mephistopheles with a jaunty, snow-tipped beard. I was almost to the door when he called after me. By my real name.

"Mr. Gall?"

"Yes." I wheeled.

"In the vehicle, you will also find a Browning Automatic rifle in good working order. We were informed that you favored the weapon."

"Thank you," I said. "Most considerate." And turning again, lengthened my stride down the long corridor. The real colonel was waiting ahead of me, at the turn to the main entrance.

As I rode back out of the palace grounds, I was meditating over the fact that the secretary had used my right name. That had been happening with increasing frequency on the last few contracts; for an agent, I seemed to be about as anonymous as Charlie Brown. I was getting a trifle long in the tooth, and my entry into any given area often started shock waves spreading. No matter what the venue, its keepers were fairly warned that I had not come for a crumpet and a chat.

Once, in fact, and not so long ago, I had sat for three weeks in a dump of a hotel in Lyons, France, dodging about like a big idiot and placing telephone calls to people I did not know. What I did during those days didn't make sense, but it wasn't intended to. I was simply a Trojan horse, planted there among the suspicious burghers and Surete agents to draw attention away from other, more meaningful operations in the area. Those water-hauls are dull work, and before that one was over even the chambermaids knew I wasn't dangerous.

My name is Joseph Liam Gall, and I come from a distinguished patrimony of Irish bogtrotters. When young, I was told that the line descended without a break from Brian Boru, but after a misspent life and some research conclude that pig-stealers and rapists would be nearer the mark. I originally came from Texas, but now claim Rhode Island when the subject arises, and at an impressionable age joined the Marine Corps.

I saw considerable action in the Pacific, in War Two, and because of incredible bravery and the fact that all ranks ahead of me were killed off, was given a field commission. In Korea I had made it up to major when I got an ankle perforated in the Changjin Reservoir retreat. It was the Chinese who had hurt me, but my real threat came from the medical sawbones who were bound to have the left foot off. I limped away from a Klamath, Oregon, hospital before those madmen could get it, and in time, with private therapy, got back nearly full motion in the ankle and foot.

Private life didn't much appeal to me, because I had spent the formative years of my life in killing people at close range. The prospect of having to claw out a country-club security by smiling at stupid bastards who would undoubtedly be adamant about buying what I had to sell seemed undesirable. Still, I was going to law school and trying to be as straight-arrow as Tom Swift when I was recruited for an intelligence agency.

The man who enlisted me captured my immediate attention by stating that I would spend most of my time "blowing up shit-houses, and stuff like that . . ." He lied, of course, but I adapted to the work. And was fortunate in having signed on when the United States was enlarging its intelligence services for the first time. Those of us who got in when the wave was breaking roamed the world like a *naïf* breed of demented Boy Scouts. We had little training in world affairs, or responsibility, but our equally ignorant leaders assured us that class would tell.

Happily, that era passed, and we began acting on more responsibly collated data. That was when we became really dangerous. True, the governments we crippled and destroyed were fascist or communist, but the touchstone was that we never replaced them with anything better. When you peeled the artichoke down to its nub, the people and systems we deep-sixed simply didn't agree with the American view, or were impeding, or threatening to impede, our access to fat market places.

Still, they were great years. A great many of us who would have made excellent elevator operators sat smoking good cigars on foreign hotel terraces while the natives grinned at the gossamer covers on these pro-consul spooks. Murder and violence continued to be done, of course, because that is the name of the game, but the results were never very lasting.

And the murders were rarely memorable for the blunt fact that very few men who choose covert work as a life's job are intelligent. They tend more to the seedy and main-chance types, and almost invariably wind up as dedicated liars. To deliberately decide to play such a game for very long indicates a basic character defect, like drug addiction or the earnest striving of missionaries who can be superior among benighted savages but not in their normal societies.

With all these things admitted, I had never regretted my choice. The work suited me. I had the physical capacity for its demands, when they came, and the mental toughness to withstand the long periods when nothing at all was happening. After several years in the field, when I had established some seniority, I came a flat ass-buster when I told some august personages that the Bay of Pigs idea could not possibly work.

When it didn't, they eased me to half-pay, and then out of the agency entirely. I bought an ancient, remote, clapboard castle on top of an Ozark hill, and remodeled it myself. I was just finishing this job when Neal Pearsall, who had been a fellow Marine officer in Korea and was now acting director of the agency's operations division, brought me back into the business, through the back door.

I became a contract counterintelligence agent, and was thus freed to choose my assignments and escaped being caught up in the bureaucratic pecking order established in Foggy Bottom. This was important, because I have a very low tolerance for fools, and would undoubtedly have been fired again if exposed to these political experts. Pearsall prevented this confrontation and repeatedly protected me in those instances in the field when I temporarily assumed that I was the latter-day incarnation of Attila the Hun.

The clapboard castle on the high Ozark hill is in mint condition now, with solid walnut furniture and all its master bedrooms *en suite* with full baths (*bidets* in Arkansas,

God save the blasphemy!). An Edo period garden fringing a thirty-foot waterfall and lagoon; an authentic teahouse near its clump of black bamboos, with Korean limestone figures set artfully among the curving flagstone walks. So that, as in any good Japanese garden, you have to bend, or turn, to find them, and so discover a new vista. . . .

An esoteric eyrie for a back-alley brigand? Right on, madam! And every bit of it: the sauna hut in the cavern under the waterfall, the mushroom beds and the tiny bonsai forests in the air-conditioned basement, the dojo gym, and the fourteen-foot timbered ceilings upstairs, were all paid for by murder.

Of strangers, individual strangers. People not known to me. I have never killed a friend in my life. And contrary to the more lurid reports, I have never been ordered by my agency to scrag anybody. They have, of course, often pointed out messy or irritating situations, caused, it was obvious, by some malcontent who should have known better. When I could not cut him off, or defuse his obstructions, I had to cut him down.

Nineteen of them, by the last count. So that you would be quite right in thinking me an amoral man, but not an undisciplined one. And if you do not want me to address your PTA meeting, madam, I will understand.

It might even be a matter for writing your Congressman, that such monsters should not only exist, but be exceedingly well paid. But before you fire off your wrathy complaint, please, investigate your Congressman, too. Like him, I am in the pay of a great state, and perhaps more effective at my job. Although it may pain and distress you, great states have no consciences.

I was in the second day of a live-pigeon shoot on a ducal estate outside Salamanca when the message reached me. This sounds as if I am cozy with nobility, but the truth is that Pepe is so hard-pressed to buy ammunition for his Hollands, much less purchase pills to support his *droit de seigneur* among the serving wenches, that each gun had entered the field at a steep price. I was trying to justify the expenses when a *Guardia Civil* officer came riding up behind my stand, leaning down from his piebald mare to hand me the message.

Pepe put me in the shooting brake immediately, and I caught a plane to Madrid. And after a long wait in that dreary airport, I flew on to Rome, Nairobi, and Johannesburg. This town has the worst vibrations of any metropolitan center in the world. Perhaps because of the honeycombed earth around it, the Rand diggings, perhaps because of the intolerable pass-controlled and regimented life of the blacks, the whole city seems to quiver under the feet, with apprehension.

At a quarter-to-four in the morning, I caught a South African Airways flight to Durban. The plane was a Viscount, almost empty, and after it had taken off I reread Neal Pearsall's cablegram. It was peremptory, and offered no clue as to what was expected of me.

JAMMED UP, the cable read. GO DURBAN SOONEST. FURTHER INSTRUCTIONS EDWARD HOTEL MARINE PARADE ROOM 324 RESERVED NAME EDWARD LAND UTMOST IMPORTANCE.

It was always of the utmost importance. Every time. I watched the lights of Johannesburg sliding under the plane's wing, and felt a slight case of the red-ass. It was a violation of my contract to be suddenly called off a holiday; I had the right to consider the problem, my part in it,

20

and to reject it if I chose. On the other hand, Pearsall so seldom hurried me in on emergency things that I had no real right to object.

The stewardess was what the Aussies call a "beaut sheila." She was small, well shaped, and had a coiled tiara of authentic sunbleached blond hair. And her friendliness was natural, something I observed by watching her deal with the few passengers ahead of me, one of whom was a Negro gentleman of middle age. He could have been a diplomat or a professor, but she leaned down into his small circle of light and made the same jokes she did with the sunburned Afrikaaners.

This pixie made it her business to try to bring me a drink, or several, but I passed because I was once a pilot on heavy aircraft and like to hear the proper responses. This is fairly foolish, since I never flew jet aircraft, but I still have a low view of sitting stoned in high-speed aircraft.

After we landed at the Durban airport, I waited for my one rawhide suitcase to come through, and caught a cab into the city. Dawn was a lightening smudge as we passed good buses in excellent repair carrying a few white passengers and other ramshackle vehicles jammed to the aisles, carrying only blacks. These latter vehicles belched noxious fumes, were obviously ill-maintained, and I had fleeting view of the expressionless black masks inhabiting them.

In the United States, we think Miami Beach is a tourist town, but we have not been advised. After clearing the center of Durban, past the massive post office, central buildings, and governmental barracks in heavy Teutonic styling, we turned left down the impressive Marine Parade. Miles and miles of high-rise luxury flats and hotels, in a curving arc around the great harbor. The aquarium, the free swimming pools, the flagged beaches which have more shark danger than any others in the world.

In the brightening dawn, my cab swung off the Parade

and into the curving drive of the Edward Hotel, which looks like a low-storied concrete barracks, inadequately painted, from the street, but is in fact one of the world's first-class hotels. I paid the driver, tipping him too much because he had had the good taste to keep his mouth shut all the way from the airport, and went into the lobby.

Things were brighter, and much more stylish, inside. I registered as Edward Land, something struck my knee, and I turned to see a small black dwarf in crimson court regalia. *Velazquez, now,* I thought, *or a South African call for Philip Morris* . . . He was grinning and pointing toward the elevators with a key attached to a huge plumb bob of zebra stripes. I followed him.

When he let me into the room upstairs, a young man of obviously American credentials was waiting. Long sideburns, Carnaby suit, and hair artfully shaggy in the back. I was tired, but knew in an instant that he was a completely up-to-date American. Groton, Harvard, fill in your own spaces, going to guide us to the new and braver world. I nodded and he got up, holding the indispensable attaché case.

"Hello, sir," he said.

"Hello," I answered, "and hush, please."

A black porter came in with my rawhide case, and I showed him where to hang it up. The gorgeously appareled dwarf danced beside me, and I gave him another dollar to get the key. When they were out, I went into the toilet, favored my two-hundred-year-old kidneys, and tried again to whirl away from that final drop. Another loser.

Going back into the bedroom, I said "Yes, sir," and the young man unzipped his attaché case and started spilling blue-backed documents onto the teak coffee table.

"You look too young to be Martin Bormann," I said, "but show me some paper."

Affronted, he showed me his plastic-contained credentials. They were impeccable, and I knew he must come from a fine family, probably in a gardened Connecticut area where you couldn't smuggle in a black man after dark, unless he was a Ph.D. and meaningful.

I handed him back the wallet containing the I.D., card. "OK. Thank you. Now fuck off."

All his sit-ins hadn't taught him the meaning of that simple phrase.

"I'm supposed to brief you, Mr. Land," he said, stammering.

"Right on," I said. "Come back and do it at eleven o'clock. I'll have the coffee heated up."

"But sir!"

"Out!" I said. "Be back here at eleven."

He went out the door with injured dignity, and I locked the door after him and had a hot and then a cold shower, trying to shake the jet tremors out of my head. And after I had toweled, fell onto the bed and into a heavy sleep.

THE young briefing agent was back at eleven. I ate breakfast while he read me the reports and dossiers on Dr. Claude Kalinga, ousted executive officer of Marundi, on the two security officers who had fled the country with him, and on the succeeding Prime Minister and strong man who had low-bridged him, General Leonhor Pangolin. The then colonel had formerly been Kalinga's Defence Minister.

My assignment, it seemed, was to take Dr. Kalinga and his two security thugs in charge, keeping them safe first in Addis Ababa and then to an undisclosed rendezvous on the west side of Lake Rudolph, in Kenya, near the Ugandan border. When the briefing agent had read all the reports through, aloud and with considerable body-English, I told him to put them back in his case.

"Where is Kalinga now?" I asked.

"In this hotel, the Georgian suite. His associates are with him."

I poured another cup of coffee. "Doesn't make sense. What are three black men, all heaved out by their own black government, doing in the best hotel in apartheid Durban?"

"That may be the reason," he said, "that they are discredited. The order to register them here came from Prime Minister Vorster's office in Praetoria. Prior to their arrival, they had been the personal guests of President Kaunda of Zambia, for over seventeen months. After Pangolin offered his million-shilling reward for the return to Marundi of Kalinga, alive, Kaunda felt he was getting to be too much of a debit.

"Kalinga requested asylum in the U.S., through our embassy in Lusaka. It was refused, but the Vorster government offered to take him on a short-term basis. Probably thought they might find some propaganda value in setting up the dialogue with black African governments that South Africa has been seeking without success."

"But Vorster is just holding him like left luggage, at our request?"

"Our informal suggestion."

"And now Vorster's enchantment is fraying, so he hollered for us to come get our package?"

"Yes, sir."

"The record shows that Dr. Kalinga is a boozer. Has he been pigging up the drink, here in the hotel, and offending delicate Afrikaaner sensibilities?"

"That's about it. The police have been to his suite twice in the last three days."

I sighed, put the coffee cup down, and poured him a cup. *They never send for me until the project starts falling apart, but I guess that's what sonsofbitches are for.*

It was a bright morning, and the beaches, walks, and formal gardens along the Marine and Snell Parades were jammed with holidaying crowds. Cruise ships and freighters were beating along offshore, past the white lighthouse. *The assignment sounded like a broken flush, playing wet nurse to an unhorsed black intellectual who had followed the pattern and become megalomanic once in office . . .*

"What's the schedule?" I asked, walking toward the bathroom.

"You have four seats reserved on Air Rhodesia's afternoon flight to Salisbury," the briefing officer said behind me. "From there at five, to Luanda, Angola. Overnight. Tomorrow morning, Pan-Am to Lisbon direct, then to Rome, and Air Ethopia to Addis Ababa."

"Good Christ!" I commented, shaking out my toothbrush, "that's halfway around the world. Why not Air Malawi or East African Airways to Nairobi, then direct into Addis?"

His reply was prompt. "Because, Mr. Land, no black government in Africa, except Ethiopia, would give Dr.

Kalinga even a transit visa. By private or public transport through their territories. Emperor Selassie agreed only because he had known Dr. Kalinga in London, but he has insisted on a very short stay in Addis and complete anonymity while there."

The more I learned, the messier it sounded. "And this meet near Lake Rudolph, which is located in a howling fucking wilderness, is it part of a coup we're cranking up, to restore this lovable tosspot to power?"

The young briefing officer's face stayed impassive behind his glasses. "I have no idea, Mr. Land. They only tell me bits and bits, never the whole story. It's aggravating as hell."

That broke me up. I shook with the first gut laugh I had had since leaving Spain. "Good on you," I said. "I went through that frustration for years. Then I found out that the reason most of the double-domes are so secretive is that they are flying in the fabled ever-diminishing concentric circles. With my own eyes, I have seen their stricken heads vanish up their own ass-holes. So let's have another touch of coffee, and go see if the Government-in-Exile of Marundi can make it to the airport vertically. If not, we'll stamp them as Judah Lion air cargo, and send them out in a van."

The ebony ex-Prime Minister turned out to be loaded, but socially so, and at a few minutes before two the five of us got out of a cab at Botha Airport. The briefing officer, who was named John Partee, hustled us all inside, gave all passports and pertinent documents to the Air Rhodesia counter, and then charged back out into the blinding sunlight to direct the avalance of the Kalinga group's baggage, which filled another cab.

The sunburned South African customs officials stared at me and my three black associates with something less than fraternal love, but the Praetoria stamp of approval on the Marundi Government-in-Exile was there, and all the requisite papers, so we were moved on down the red-arrowed line to the waiting room. As a matter of fact, since I had no official connection with the Kalinga party, they were shown swiftly through the diplomatic lane while I struggled along with the peasants.

I joined them in the cool waiting room just in time to see one of Kalinga's security men buying three quarts of Bell's 12-Year-Old Special Scotch at the duty-free shop. Fortunately, the order would not be delivered until we were boarding. John Partee, winded with headlong activities on our behalf, came to sit beside me and point out the results of his labors.

The overweight on Dr. Kalinga's luggage and personal effects, together with that of his associates, from Durban to Salisbury to Luanda to Lisbon to Rome to Addis Ababa, had amounted to over seventeen-hundred U.S. dollars. This, although Partee, who was rapidly turning into an alert boy, had managed to have the bulk of it shipped on from Luanda as unaccompanied luggage. Straight through to Addis, while we overnighted. Still, as he handed me the receipts, I had that faint tremor in my bowels, one that often precedes bad dysentery.

For years in the field, I had seen this same offhand profligacy with the docile U.S. taxpayer's money. For just such causes. And for years I had been waiting for someone, some league, some Nader-like prober, to scream, "What is this imbecility?" No one ever had. I pocketed the receipts, thanked Partee, and in a few minutes our flight to Salisbury, Rhodesia, was called.

Walking out the gate and onto the steaming tarmac toward the ancient Viscount, I waved back once to Partee and thought idly that it was a pleasant terminal but grotesquely insufficient for a metropolis like Durban. Dr. Kalinga was walking ahead of me, bantering with his associates, and I had to admit that his tailor was good. The exuberant little black man wore a bowler hat and carried a neatly furled umbrella.

Since I had all the tickets, I stayed close behind them. There was inevitable jostling on the loading ramp, and because Dr. Kalinga and his two friends were the only black passengers, brittle and not-so-well-bred comments began. Except for eight spacious seats in the front of the old Viscount, of which we had tickets for four, one whole side of the aisle, the other seating was three-and-two and the avenue between them crowded.

The loading passengers were chattering Aryan teenagers, returning from South African prep schools and universities for the "long vac," Rhodesian planters, government officials, and the usual ebullient salesmen from the Levant. These latter were slickly dressed and amiable; when the last atomic trump is blown they will come crawling to the edge of the devastated areas with perfectly useless but plausible instruments to delay radiation death.

There were also the inevitables: the American tourists. Teachers past their bloom, having decided they would never be raped in Milwaukee, no matter how much they tempted fate; retired dentists from Michigan, who took a little laughing gas at every stop, and the inevitable full-haired hippies, in moccasins and jeans, girls only detectable from the boys if you grabbed them by the tits, and then not always. They were young, bland, and so determined to be different that they turn out to be as homogenized as IBM staffers.

For several years, every time I left the country on a contract, I had encountered teenaged, liberated America abroad in increasing swarms. In their pursuit of doing their thing, they had rendered conversation unnecessary. I could have taped a ten-minute cassette of their underground responses, and it could have been played by any of them, meeting any other of them, from Tierra del Fuego to Milford Sound, New Zealand . . .

Things got edgier as I pressed behind my black associates up toward the only first-class oasis in the Air Rhodesia plane. A blond stewardess was trying to get us through, finally did, and when we had settled in around the four wide seats and the table up front, angry murmurings came floating up to us. Dr. Kalinga looked across at me, I shook my head to indicate silence, and even his beetle-browed security men seemed wilted into their funereal suite.

It was an unavoidable, sweaty proximity. Rhodesia had not suffered much from the British sanctions and blockades, and in many ways its economy had prospered. But it was still short of petrol products, and had not been able to afford new aircraft. This ancient Viscount, a fine aircraft in its day, had no blowers working in it. The boarding had been delayed; the all-white contingent of passengers, and my three black charges, were all irritated.

I was hoping to Christ, without blasphemy, that the pilots would crank up the prop-jet fans and cool us all off when the door to the pilot's enclosure opened. The four-striper, the captain himself, came out. Settling his braided flight cap on his sun-cured blond hair, walking past us briskly, saying in a conversational tone, "Please evacuate the aircraft immediately. Please evacuate the aircraft immediately . ."

Dr. Kalinga glanced at me again, removing his visorlike sunglasses, and I said, "Sit still."

The three stewardesses began advising everyone to leave the aircraft and to take their personal belongings with them, and the five-abreast tiers of seats started hurtling into the narrow aisle. Banging handbags, hats, cameras, souvenirs into each other. While we sat motionless in the front seats, the copilot and radio operator joined the surging crowds, shrugging uniform coats over their short-sleeved shirts.

Dr. Kalinga was alarmed. He spoke to his two thugs in Swahili, with emphasis, and leaned over the table. "Perhaps there is danger. Shouldn't we go?"

"Get your personal belongings in hand," I said, "including your whiskey, and sit still."

After what seemed like a long time, but was really only several minutes, the ill-tempered shovings in the aisle lessened, and I led the Government-in-Exile out the back of the plane and down the ramp. We joined the crowd straggling toward the blossom-covered air terminal. When we were approaching the waiting room, young John Partee came out to meet us.

He was ready to question me, but I told Dr. Kalinga to take his friends inside and be seated. That I would soon join them. When they were through the doorway, I asked Partee if he had a security contact at the airport. He said yes, and in a few minutes came back with one of the sun-bronzed blonds in a short-sleeved white shirt. I asked why the aircraft had been evacuated.

"Bit of a drag, really," he drawled, and I wondered where he had picked that phrase up, since there is no television in South Africa, although they have plans to debase themselves later. "Fact is, the evacuation was routine. You see, when someone books for a flight, has baggage put on it, but does not board, we automatically evacuate. We were ready to close this flight, but someone had checked in baggage, and did not appear . . ."

He was explaining the procedure patiently when the Viscount was ripped apart by explosions, three of them. I was hurled forward off my feet, caromed into Partee, and grabbed at the South African security man before I fell into the wall of the terminal. As I was pushing erect, a fourth racking explosion shook the burning, disjointed plane, and debris hurtling from it began to shower down around us and onto the roof of the terminal.

Something cool dripped onto my hands as I shoved away from the wall, and I found that I was bleeding from the mouth. Using my handkerchief, I wiped it and my hands, and told Partee, who had been flung back into the rhododendron bushes, to get us a cab before the rush began.

Going back into Durban, I discovered that one of my molar caps had been jarred loose, causing the bleeding. Since I had two of these elegant devices, and both had cost only a thousand dollars, I was only five hundred dollars hurt. What I was most worried about was pain in the nerve, covered by the inner cap, but it did not show up. On the way in, I told Partee we had to have one of the agency's safe houses, and quick.

The Government-in-Exile sat in the back of the cab clutching their individual quarts of now-illegal Bell's Best Old Scotch Whisky. "Afore ye go . . . ," it said on the top label. In a subdued voice, Dr. Kalinga asked if it might be permissible, in view of everything, if they could open one of the bottles?

"Man," I said, "I think it's mandatory."

I heard the foil being broken, and prolonged gurglings.

We rode into the center of Durban, and Kalinga leaned forward and said, "Do you think they were trying to kill *me,* Mr. Land?"

"No question about it," I answered, and he leaned back. There were further gurglings. The safe house turned out to be, after a telephone stop for Partee, two adjoining apartments in the Golden Sands Holiday Hotel. On the tenth floor, overlooking the Snell Parade. They were completely furnished, had kitchens and all utensils and china, silverware, and stocked pantries and refrigerators.

An English gentleman named Mr. Alexander appeared briefly to let us in, and seemed more owner of the huge building overlooking the sea than manager. When we had settled Kalinga and his men into one of the apartments, John Partee and I opened the seaside windows of the other one. I put the pot on to boil, and asked John how he had booked the tickets on the flight to Salisbury. He flinched, but said in the names of Land, Kalinga, and associates. The bookings had been made the day before, soon after Partee learned when I would arrive.

While I made the cups of instant coffee, he looked disconsolate, and said, "I guess I really blew it, didn't I?"

"Not entirely," I said, handing him his cup. "Now you can stop payment on all that excess baggage."

A couple of hours later, after we had taken the juice of a quart of Black Jack Daniel's, I had Partee go downstairs to watch the apartment-hotel switchboard operator while I placed a call to Neal Pearsall, in Washington. Calculating the time difference, I knew he would be at his home in Maryland, and I had not time to seek out a scrambler phone. Partee could at least see that the downstairs operator kept his key closed after we were connected.

Neal had been asleep, and bad-tempered. When I told him that the plane reservations for my black party, to one of the few lily-white countries left in Africa, had set up a bomb demolition of the plane, he grunted.

"Your style, Joe. You are the classic disaster man. I ask you to escort a simple African dipsomaniac from square one to square two, so naturally we have a disaster."

"You also violated my contract agreement, and jerked me away from a holiday without warning. If you want this fellow taken to Addis, and from there to Lake Rudolph, I will do it. But not with these two private thugs of his. And we cannot get to Addis, as you know, by any ordinary air route."

"Okay. What do you want?"

"I want a military plane for a direct flight from here to Ethiopia. It can be small, because most of His ex-Excellency's luggage went up in flames on the Durban airport."

"Right. We have some light bombers visiting Kenya, I think. Might be able to detach one of them. Hang on . . ." He left the phone and I knew he was checking the big wall map in his office. "Yes."

"When?"

"In the morning. Do you like Partee?"

"Only because he knows what fradulent pricks you executives are."

"That's the spirit. A trendy boy, pure hatred for the Establishment. I'll start working on your transport now." He hung up, and when Partee came back from his vigil on the switchboard I gave him another drink. Then he went home, wherever that was in Durban, and I collapsed on another strange bed.

By midafternoon the next day, Dr. Kalinga and I were in the high Ethiopian capital. As we registered in the Ghion Hotel, I could smell aromatic eucalyptus leaves burning, and could see the bomber which had ferried us up from Durban blasting back into the sky.

WHEN the long sedan entered the Ghion grounds, the colonel said something briskly in Amharic, and the car went past the front entrance and circled to the back of the hotel. Or the back of the main structure; the Ghion had several wings and a large conical bar and dining room. At this juncture of structures, a khaki-colored Toyota Land-Cruiser was waiting with its lights out. When the colonel got out of the Mercedes, two soldiers hurried out of its front seat and snapped to attention.

He returned their salute, and motioned me forward to stand beside him. Then he instructed them briskly; their eyes swept briefly over me with the dark faces still set ahead.

"I have told them," said the colonel in English, "that they are to take you, a black man from East Africa, and an Ethiopian nurse to the Kenya border. I did not say where, because if the Somali tribesmen in the Northern Frontier District are raiding, you may not be allowed into Kenya below Kelam, which is the Lake Rudolph route. In that event, you may have to go east to Moyale, the larger border post. Sometimes, even if there is trouble, the Kenyan government will provide armed guards there."

"Thank you," I said.

He walked to the back end of the Land Cruiser, opened it, and asked me to check the armament provided. I did, and found that it was exactly as the Emperor's secretary had promised. In addition to the weapons and ammunition, the back section of the rugged four-wheel-drive vehicle was loaded with racked petrol cans, water cans, and boxed chlorine tablets to purify any more we would pick up, Ethiopian Army route food rations, four new spike-treaded tires, and other parts and supplies I could not make out.

When I withdrew my head, the colonel slammed the rear hatch down, and asked how soon I would be ready to leave the hotel; adding before I could answer that the Toyota had been fully serviced, and that there was enough petrol in the auxiliary tins for a thousand kilometers, although we should not need to touch that for the first day. It was not a very subtle hint; I remembered the dapper little secretary's unequivocal direction that we should drive for twenty-four hours without break, after leaving Addis Ababa.

"I can be ready in twenty minutes, Colonel," I said. "Dr. Kalinga may take somewhat longer, but I will do my best to hurry him."

He nodded, and said that porters would be waiting in the corridor outside the suite. Then glanced at his wristwatch, and said that if our party had not cleared the hotel grounds in an hour and a half, he and his men would be glad to assist in our departure. His tone was not threatening, but I read the message, thanked him again, and went up to the suite.

When I knocked on the door of Dr. Kalinga's bedroom, it was opened by Maryam, the unsmiling Danakil girl. The bedroom itself was dark, except for a shaded light in the bathroom beyond. I explained to Maryam that we had to pack and leave immediately. She replied that she would get everything ready, that Dr. Kalinga was sleeping. But in an hour he would be ready to travel, although some help might be required in getting him to the car.

"Is he passed out?" I asked harshly. Her dark profile, clean as Nefertiti's, went to one side, in question. She did not understand the phrase. "Has he had too much drink to walk?"

"No. But he would not eat, insisted on ordering more *tej*, so I allowed him a little, with a sleeping potion in it. He will be all right."

I nodded to Kalinga's nurse-cum-contract-wife, and

said that I would return in half an hour. Maryam was turning back into the darkened bedroom when I asked if she had eaten. She shrugged and said there had been no time, with all the excitement. I said I was going to the upstairs lounge bar, and would have something sent down for her.

My own packing took ten minutes, because I had only the small leather bag John Partee had provided me in Durban, with its scanty supply of new underwear, socks, and toilet articles. My big rawhide bag, which I had traveled with for seventeen years, had gone up, or apart, in the exploding Viscount. I put its successor in the hall, and one of the soldiers, not porters as the Colonel had said, immediately grabbed it and took off for the elevator.

The roof bar was glass-walled on three sides, and an outside terrace went all around it. Every seat in the place had a superb view of downtown Addis Ababa, but for some unknown reason a transparent scrim of cloth hung all around the glass, so that the legendary city outside was filtered through this useless curtain. I ordered a filet steak *au poivre* and a half-bottle of red wine sent down to Miss Lalibela in the suite, and ordered myself a shashlik and a large bottle of Tuborg.

I was working on the good beer, waiting for the shashlik, when two figures drifted in front of me, outside on the narrow terrace and distorted by the filmy curtain. As I lighted a small Holland cigar, the couple went into a clinch of some extremity.

The girl was tiny, not much more than five feet, and wore a tight sweater which I could almost decipher through the see-through curtain. She was shapely, had long, smooth hair, and wore black hot pants which were cut high above the curve of her buttocks. I thought her dress singularly inappropriate for after dark, in one of the best hotels in Addis, but then I was a stranger there myself.

Her companion was a tall Ethiopian boy in much more

formal attire. As I sipped my beer, he locked his left arm behind her back, drawing her up on her tiptoes, and began to kiss her with slow and satyrlike precision. His right hand was plunged down inside the front of her provocative hot pants, moving with urgency.

I was annoyed. First, because they had chosen to stand not three feet from me, just beyond the glass wall, and secondly, because the Ethiopian boy had deliberately turned her so that his gropings could be observed by everybody in the rooftop bar. There was a solid blank wall behind the bar and grill, to which they could have repaired when in heat without being observed.

Oh Christ, I told myself irritably, *you just envy the boy, obviously a product of the Ethiopian country-club set, perhaps the son of a Ras or duke, and hence privileged in this ancient kingdom. While you have a problem of considerable magnitude, feel the gut tickle of incipient dysentery, and although reasonably sound are not a real candidate to take the place, at your age, Father William, of the arrogant young lecher outside the glass. . . .*

After the long and exhibitionistic embrace, the tall boy dropped her, ran his hands up under the tight sweater over her firm young breasts, and the tiny girl arched her back. Her long hair was trailing over her forehead, and when she threw her head aimlessly and glanced through the glass at me I saw that her eyes were dazed.

While I poured more beer, pretending not to notice, the young Ethiopian grandee laughed, withdrew his hands from under the sweater, and led her off down the terrace. With her head locked under his right elbow. She followed trotting, head down at a queer angle, and twice before they vanished around the turn to the blank wall, seemed trying to free herself.

My shashlik came, I unspeared it, and began to eat. The little vignette involving the tiny girl still rankled; I could not rationalize it away. What they had done was not unusual, except that it should have been done in a room with the door closed. "Tend your own garden, kid," I admonished myself, and gnawed away at the spiced nuggets of beef, which had too much oil on them.

Twenty minutes later, I had finished and was walking down the stairs to the German elevators when the tiny girl came bursting out of a room with the tight sweater nearly torn off her shoulders. She was barefooted, and the hot pants were ripped on one side. When I stepped into the small elevator, she cried, "Wait!" and came running to join me. I pressed the fourth-floor button, and we descended.

She was standing facing away from me, crying bitterly, and there were angry scratches along her smooth young back. I made her at about nineteen, not more than twenty, but did not comment as the elevator sighed to a halt at four.

"Oh, God!" she cried, turning around and trying, ineffectually, to cover her breasts under the ripped sweater, which had been bought by her to show them off. She had been brutalized, but the nipples were still up. The mascara and too-blue eyeshadow she employed to make her a full-fledged woman seemed to have worked too well. Somebody, probably the arrogant young Ethiopian aristocrat, had turned her out, after she had asked for it.

She was all atremble, and her plea tumbled out in pure midwestern Bible Belt anguish. "Please help me," she sobbed, "I don't know anyone here . . ."

You took a few provocative turns before finding that out, I thought, *like deliberately unveiling your breasts and wearing those silly hot pants.* But I opened the door to the elevator and told her to get down the hall, fast, and turn into Room 410. As she sprinted away, I saw that her bare feet were dirty and stained.

I was carrying four bottles of brandy I had bought in the bar, and when I had locked the door behind me opened one and got two glasses from the table. One I filled with water from the carafe, and the other I loaded with two inches of the brandy. She was whimpering in the chair next to the terrace; I took both glasses to her and watched while she tossed the brandy off neat and refused the chaser.

"All right," I said, "I've got about ten minutes. I'm on urgent business, getting ready to leave this hotel. So talk up a storm, and try not to lie."

The little girl whose organs had outgrown her head began to talk like a metronome gone crazy. Her name was Dorothy Tyson, and her father was a district supervisor for the telephone company, in Joplin, Missouri. Did I know what a drag life was in Joplin, Missouri? I didn't interrupt, just let her run. It would do her no good to know that I owned a tall hill with a big house on it, in the Ozark Mountains not far from her home, and that I had often shopped in Joplin for hardware while reconstructing the house.

She and her friend, Betsy Newman, who was from near Joplin, had taken a Pan-Am 27-day excursion flight to Nairobi, Kenya, and had used the optional part of their tickets to go further down to Malawi. In Blantyre, they had been arrested while wearing miniskirts down the main street, and deported back to Nairobi by personal order of President Blanda.

They hadn't liked anything in Kenya, except the Thorn Tree lounge in the New Stanley Hotel, but the black boys there had been so *hateful*. If they bought you a sandwich, they expected you to ball. Anywhere. On the main street, in a doorway or a car, just to prove that being black was beautiful. . . .

She and Betsy had cabled their parents for more money, saying they were doing a seminar on African Studies at the University of Nairobi, and then had flown to Addis.

It was beginning to sound like a teenager's disjointed life. I had a brandy myself, and told her to telescope the story.

"Well, we got a room at the YWCA, and met two off-duty U.S. Army guys from Asmara. They took us to this bar place, and we were drinking *tej,* and these two Ethiopian guys came over and sat down with us. I don't know what happened, but after a while the Americans were gone. The Ethiopian boys said we would come here to the Ghion, and have a party."

"Look, kid," I said, wondering what I could do with this nubile derelict. "I don't have much time—"

"Okay, okay. I think they must have dropped some hash in our drinks, up in the piazza. Don't even remember getting here, but I do remember two of them putting it to Betsy, and she was screaming up a storm. They were working her out at both ends. Then Mr. Ato, the guy you saw me with on the terrace, dragged me into the other room, and punched me around and balled me good.

"When I tried to get away, he knocked me down and called the other stud in from the room where Betsy had been. But she wasn't there anymore. I tried to fight them off, but they had a real gang-bang. You know, laughing. And then they went out and I called the YWCA, but the people said Betsy was in jail, and the police had picked up our baggage and everything. Even our passports."

She was blubbering again, and I gave her a half drink. I had no idea what to do with her. Time after time after time, in many countries, I had seen her like. *We are the new, free breed from the U.S.A., flouting all your local customs, but you must not try to . . . really . . . do that to us.* While wearing the most inflammatory clothing and swishing their butts around. Now they had invaded even the ancient highlands of Africa, where a woman was used for procreation, and often the most acceptable sex partner was a young boy.

What could I do with her, this wretched little manhandled girl who had gotten too much of what she had come for. Call the American Embassy? That would blow me, because the phones were undoubtedly tapped by the Emperor's intelligence services. *Mr. Ato had ravished her, had he?* Didn't the stupid little girl know that *Ato* was only the ceremonial title for "mister," like *U* in Burma? So she had been turned out by "mister."

On the other hand, if I pieced her off with a few dollars, and wished her good luck, with her passport in the hands of the police, it was not inconceivable that she might go down the ancient slave route to the Red Sea. They could drug her and abuse her into a coma en route, and while she wouldn't be worth as much, in the Aden area, as a handsome young boy, further on into the Trucial States or Saudi Arabia she might bring a handsome price.

I had enough on my plate. Who cares about violated daughters from Joplin, Missouri, U.S.A.?

My revery was disturbed by a pounding on the suite door. I went to open it, and found myself facing the arrogant Ethiopian youth who had been manhandling Dorothy on the terrace. He looked toward the girl huddled in the chair, and said, "I think you've got something of mine."

She ran out onto the terrace. And he made a mistake; he pushed me aside. I turned from the force of it, planted my right foot, and hit him so hard that he somersaulted. He simply turned a flip, because I hooked a right hand under his ear that turned him over completely. His Italian shoes were curled under him as he lay.

I walked through the sitting room of the suite, knocked on the door of Kalinga's bedroom, and it was opened again by Maryam. I told her what had happened, asked if she could immobilize the young Ethiopian I had knocked out, and she nodded. Behind her, I could see Claude Kalinga sitting up and taking tea. He was uninterested. She got a medical bag, followed me across the sitting room into the other room, and knelt beside the unconscious boy.

Deftly, she hit him with a hypodermic shot in the upper arm. Both of us carried his limp figure into one of the big closets, and closed the door on him.

I called out, "Dorothy!" and the tiny girl came in off the terrace. I told Maryam that she had to be more suitably clothed, and that we would pick her up at the entrance to the hotel grounds. The Danakil girl nodded, and led her off toward the other bedroom.

Fortunately, Dr. Kalinga was no problem. He walked to the elevator and back to the waiting Land-Cruiser under his own power. All the way, he was humming, "Underneath the Arches," which he was too young to remember. It must have been taught to him by an old witch doctor. When we had left the shadows in back of the hotel, and swung down the circular drive, I ordered the driver to stop at the entrance to the swimming pool.

When the Land-Cruiser stopped, I got out and was almost knocked down by Dorothy Tyson of Joplin, Missouri. She came out of a clump of banana trees at speed. Her torn mod clothes had been replaced by a modest black shift dress, with a white silk *shamma* that looked like the one Maryam Lalibela had been wearing the first time I had seen her, standing beside Dr. Kalinga's bed.

We were out of sight from the Ghion Hotel's impressive entrance. I had always known, since listening to the Emperor's secretary, that the driver-guide was absolutely indispensable. The other corporal, in the front seat beside the driver, I also knew to be a palace spy. When we let Dorothy squeeze in between us, in the second seat, he turned angrily and began a harangue that was part Amharic and part English.

I had anticipated this, and fed him the best part of a sock with a bar of soap in it. He collapsed in mid-cry, and I carried him back into the banana grove. This left us with a wild-eyed driver, who became considerably more docile after I tilted a carbine under his left earlobe. Under such gentle suasion, he drove us through Addis Ababa. Past and around the lighted towers of the capital.

When we got to the outskirts, and he had turned down the principle highway south, I let him feel the carbine muzzle again and ordered him to turn off onto the alternate road. He braked and protested volubly, but another

carbine-twitch changed his direction. We left the hard-sur-
faced road and went down the dirt track.

I had to do it the hard way, because with world-traveler
Dorothy aboard, we had directly crossed the Ethiopian
police and they would be looking for us, as well as General Pangolin's *shiftas*. And if the corporal I had dumped
into the banana grove was ambulatory, the Palace and the
Ethiopian military would have joined the chase.

The American girl, whose presence represented the stup-
idest idea I had had in several centuries, was sprawled
between Maryam and myself. She was sleeping peacefully
with her head in the Danakil's lap and her bare dirty feet
over my knees. As we rolled south, toward the Kenyan
border, I glanced at Maryam. She was staring out the window on her side.

THE Land Cruiser went rolling south, occasionally slamming into a pothole. I studied the road map. Fortunately, it was official, had come with the vehicle, and showed the frequent check points where the finance guards stopped all vehicles. Most of these were on the all-weather road to Awassa, which we had left and were paralleling on the dry-weather track to Assela and Adaba. That distance was roughly three hundred kilometers. After we had covered it, we then had to strike almost due west and bypass Awassa.

The Ethiopian driver was expert at the wheel, but I was sure he would turn the key on us at the first opportunity. He knew the roads, presumably even the side tracks, or else the Palace would not have assigned him to take us to Kenya border. And in thinking of the Palace, I could imagine the quiet fury of the Emperor's young private secretary, the one who had such a passion for neatness. He would by now have sent the word cracking down to every remote post in south Ethiopia.

Because I had crossed him up good, after he had treated me fairly. I had deliberately blown his game plan sky high, even though it had been constructed to help us. I didn't even know who the young Ethiopian sporting type was, the one I had slugged and put to bed in the Ghion closet. And I had probably compromised Maryam Lalibela, who had given him the sedative shot. Then I remembered that she would not be involved, because the sporting type had been completely out before she hit him with the shot.

In addition, there had been the corporal whom I had slugged and laid to rest in the banana grove at the fork of the Ghion drive. And finally, young violated Dorothy from Joplin, Missouri, who had no clothes, no passport, and no

45

exit permit to leave Ethiopia. I had the portfolio which held all necessary documents for Dr. Kalinga, myself, and Maryam Lalibela. But little old Dorothy was strictly from hunger, trying to make it the hard way in the Kingdom of Sheba.

I had been tracing our route by flashlight, and switched it off. Folding the map, I lighted a cigar and in the brief flame from my lighter noticed that Dorothy was still sleeping; Dr. Kalinga was dozing against the door opposite the driver, and Maryam was staring ahead. I could tell little about the character of the country we were passing through, because the night was overcast. At corners, the Toyota's headlights swept across juniper firs, the green blades of banana trees, and the grey-green profusion of towering eucalyptus groves.

The Emperor's secretary would be quite right to try and halt, even imprison, us. He represented the second generation of Emperor Haile Selassie's long struggle to bring his remote mountain empire into the twentieth century. Beginning in 1916, when he was Ras Tafari Makonnen, regent and heir-apparent to Empress Zauditu, the little man had begun selecting the brightest young men in Ethiopia for foreign schooling, principally in England.

That dream had ended in 1937, after the Italians had occupied his empire and he was exiled. An attempt had been made on the life of the Fascist Italian General Graziano, by Ethiopian patriots. In retaliation, most of that thin line of selected, foreign-trained Ethiopians had been put to death, a good many of them being hurled alive out of Italian military aircraft. So the young palace secretary I had met represented the second attempt at an elitist ruling corps for the Negus' country.

After we had driven for two hours, Dorothy's bare feet jerked across my lap and she sat up, yawning. Rubbing at her eyes, she stretched and asked where we were, for God's sake. I said I had no idea, for God's sake. Somewhere in southern Ethiopia. She laughed and fumbled in the skirt pocket of the black shift dress. Took out a small tin, produced a bulky cigarette, and asked me for a light.

I flipped my lighter, and she took a deep drag and sighed, leaning back. After she had inhaled a few more lungsful of smoke, the inside of the Land-Cruiser began to smell like a vulcanizing shop on overtime. I shook my head in wonder. The world traveler from Joplin had lost what remained of her virtue, had blown her passport and her luggage, but had somehow held onto her supply of pot. She sucked away until the tip of the roach glowed, and I thought we might all get a minimal contact high just out of her air pollution.

"Look, old dad," she said to me, squinting through smoke skeins, "I hate to be a drag, but it's like I have to make that used-beer scene. You know? So could you maybe ask Sammy Davis to pull off the road for a minute?"

I tapped the driver on the shoulder. When he half-turned his head, I told him to stop. Maryam had not been to sleep at all, and as the cruiser halted, Dr. Kalinga roused and knuckled his eyes sleepily. I told them that we would have coffee, and sandwiches, and they could attend to any other problems they had during the twenty-minute halt.

Dorothy pushed past me and went gambolling into the shadows. Just as quickly, she came back, trying to adjust her dress. "Goddamned lions or something in there!" she shouted, pointing toward the grove of fig trees she had hastily vacated. I doubted lions, and in a few seconds, three jackals came prowling out of the darkness and stood sillhouetted in the Toyota's headlight beams, unafraid, with their eyes green slits.

Dr. Kalinga laughed, and even the driver smiled. The wraiths vanished back into the shadows, and we poured coffee, still hot in the thermos jars, and ate sandwiches packed by the Ghion Hotel. All standing outside the vehicle, with its doors open, using the seats as tables.

The leaden sky had lightened; the moon was trying to break through the overcast and partially succeeding. There were dark mountain ramparts visible to the east and west. I knew that the Ethiopian guerrillas had operated through this area while returning Haile Selassie to power. the little Emperor had been restored to his throne by Orde Wingate, that eccentric and underrated military genius who had later been killed in a plane crash in north Burma, not far from the Upper Assam station from which I had been flying cargo into Chancre Jack's China.

When our light repast was over, Dr. Kalinga and I sauntered into the fig grove Dorothy had vacated so incontinently for a friendly neighborhood piss. As we stood there with our backs to the Land-Cruiser, I asked the little black man, still debonair even in his rumpled clothes, how he felt.

"Miserable, thanks," he said cheerfully, in his clipped British accent. "Just miserable. But I expect that's because I'm not very intelligent, really. I *will* swill down the stuff, you know. And one day it will kill me. Quite dead. Death, you know, is nature's way of telling us to slow down."

I laughed involuntarily, and nearly lost my grip on the plumbing. "Doctor," I said, "you're the best of two cultures, and a man of learning. Your country, and this whole continent of Africa, needs the few people like you who can direct them."

Kalinga sighed and buttoned his fly. For him, nothing so plebian as a zipper; his Savile Row tailors had seen to that. "Then you don't believe I'm a monster? I've done very bad things, you know."

"I am not competent to discuss that," I answered, zipping up my own pants. "It is my job to take you to a meeting in the Lake Rudolph area. It would help a great deal if you drank less on the way, because we might be ambushed by *shiftas* hired by General Pangolin. My bringing along this foolish American hippie girl will cause further trouble

with the Ethiopian authorities. I had no right to add that
to your burdens."

"Oh . . ." The little black dandy took a spotless handkerchief from his inside jacket pocket, spat on it, and pro-
ceeded to scrub at his face and hands. "The young lady
seems not overly bright, it is true. But she is, like myself, a
stateless person, so we must do what we can for her."

He offered me the handkerchief, and I declined, saying
that Maryam, his nurse and short-term *damoz* wife, was a
deal more attractive. That if he boxed the decanters less,
he might find considerable solace in her.

It was Kalinga's turn to laugh. "You are a natural-born
courtier, Mr. Land," he said. "I often heard such sugges-
tions when I was in power, but I think you have no ulteri-
or motive. Other than the meeting at Lake Rudolph, that
is. And Mistress Maryam is desirable, as you infer. However, I fear that she is stronger than I am."

"But the *damoz* rights——"

He buttoned his jacket with trembling fingers. "Mr.
Land, do you not yet know the ephemeral quality of contracts with women? I have had one white wife, and seven
black ones. I am a failed politician with a price of a million shillings on my head, driven out of exile in Zambia
and being conducted by an agent of the United States to a
dubious rendezvous at Lake Rudolph. You will pardon me
if my testicular excitement is not as active as that of an
Eton schoolboy."

He had put the matter with far more succinctness than I
had dared. We were walking back toward the faint lights
in the interior of the Land-Cruiser, listening to Dorothy's
laughter, when someone started firing at us through the
headlight beams from the other side of the road. They
were using an automatic rifle set to single fire, and it
stitched up the soft pumice earth around our feet.

I was carrying the carbine under my left elbow, with the
safety off. With my right arm, I slammed Dr. Kalinga to

the ground and went with him, shouting for those in th
Toyota to cut its lights. They went off abruptly, and I la
with my face half in leaf mold, listening to the stillness c
the Ethiopian night. We all listened.

The sky overhead had gone to broken, and the emerg
ing moon put a sheen of silver across the vehicle standin;
at the side of the road, with its doors open. No further fir
ing or sound came from across the road, which wa
fringed by arching bamboos. Still, we waited. The nigh
sounds began to come back slowly; a tentative frog, :
hoarse nightjar's call.

I pushed up to my elbows, cradling the carbine. "Don'
move," I whispered to Kalinga. "Don't raise your head, o
move at all." Then I began to snake toward the Land-
Cruiser on my elbows, holding the carbine ahead of me.
When I got to the vehicle, I repeated, "Don't move at all,"
to the three figures on the ground around it. And went on
crawling around the back of the Toyota.

The rough track of the road was too bright with moonlight for me to navigate on my belly. So I took a deep
breath and took it crouching, as fast as I could. I thought I
had it made, and was nearly to the bamboo shade when
the hidden rifle erupted again. I fell forward into the
grove, with edged fronds sawing at me, and raked the
place where I had seen the muzzle flashes erupting. The
rifle cracked again, slashing at the fronds around me, and I
spent the rest of the clip.

I ejected it and rammed a fresh one in. There could be
no silent stalking now; the bamboo rustled every time I
moved. So I went forward crouching and spraying fire.
One man bolted out of the grove, running toward the
Toyota, and I crossed him belt-high. He jackknifed down,
groaning, and tried to get up again. Two head shots finished him, and the rifle dropped from his hands.

My feet were submerged in marshy turf. The firing had
silenced the night sounds again. Forcing myself to count in
my head, but thousands, as artillery men used to do while

cutting fuses, I allowed five minutes and a bit to go by. There was no rustle from the bamboo ahead.

I moved cautiously into it. After I had taken a few steps, my right ankle nearly turned. I had stepped on a man's arm. I stood over him with the carbine ready, and flipped him over with my right boot. He flopped limply. Spreading his arms, I knelt and found his rifle with its butt submerged in the boggy earth. Then, standing on his outspread hands, I called for Kalinga to bring me the flashlight-torch from the Toyota, but not to turn it on until I gave him the word.

The rotund little African came running across the moonlit road, and I waited with the motionless man's hands sinking beneath my feet. Kalinga paused, uncertain, at the edge of the bamboo grove, and I called for him to turn on the torch. He flicked its beam around and came thrusting through the green tubes toward me. He was a failed Prime Minister, but the little black man had guts enough.

While he pointed the way with the torch's beam, I dragged the man who had been under my feet onto the road. The muddy ground sighed as it released its hold on him. When I had placed him beside the other one, cut down while running across the road, I took the torch and played it across both bodies, praying that they would not be wearing Ethiopian military uniforms.

They weren't. Both had on dark, ill-fitting suits. The one who had tried to escape across the road was bleeding still from the abdomen and the right side of his head was shattered. The other had two wounds in the face, but neither seemed important enough to be fatal, until I turned him over. The back of his coat was drenched with blood from hits in the low back. Both had negroid features, and were obviously not Ethiopians.

I switched off the torch and asked, "*Shiftas,* Dr. Kalinga?"

"No," he said, anger in his voice. "General Pangolin's men. They used to be in my C.I.D. Division."

"Oh?" And I wondered how many times he had sent them on murderous errands like this, to mud huts or foreign embassies. "In that case, we'd better put them back in the bamboos. You take the lightest one . . ." And I began to drag one of the corpses back toward the grove, by his heels.

"But," protested Kalinga, "they must have come in a vehicle. There might be more of them. Shouldn't we locate their transport?"

"We don't have that kind of time, Doctor," I explained. "We have to bypass Awassa before daylight. If anyone else was with them, they don't seem to be very brave comrades. And I heard hyenas coughing on the other side of the road, so they'll be taken care of before morning. Let's get on with it, shall we?"

When we had dragged the two corpses into the bamboo grove, we went back across the road to the Land-Cruiser. I told the driver that I would take the wheel for the next four hours and he burst into a tirade. The gist of it was that he was never to relinquish the driver's job.

I loaded Dr. Kalinga, Maryam, and Dorothy into the second seat and asked the driver if he would rather wait in the bamboos, while the hyenas came to visit. He shook his head and touched the rough silver pectoral cross hanging from his neck. I motioned him to the far side of the front seat and was examining the map by the dashboard lights when Dorothy fired up another marijuana cigarette. Its pungent aroma began filling the interior of the Toyota again.

"Wow!" she said, "This is exciting."

I turned and slapped the bulky cigarette out of her hand. "Kid," I said slowly, "you're not even a free rider here. You are just an embarrassment who may get us all killed or jailed. Keep your mouth shut, and quit perfuming the truck until I can find some place to dump you.

Two men have just been killed. They're dead over there, and soon the hyenas will eat them. It's not another stanza of 'Peyton Place.' "

I started the Land-Cruiser and drove off down the moonlit road, south. Dorothy was crying indignantly, and the hyenas were beginning their barking whoops, slinking in around the bamboo grove. Before long, we would have to strike west at Adaba, and try to get by Awassa, and the finance posts, before dawn.

As I guided the bouncing Toyota down the cratered road, I was thinking that the driver was the problem. I hadn't told Kalinga, or anyone else, but my delivery date on him, to the Lake Rudolph rendezvous, was less than seventy-two hours away. There we were to meet a man who would stage us further, but I had no idea where that would lead. As the Emperor's secretary had said, from that remote area we could take our choice of The Sudan, Uganda, or Kenya.

But not unless we could lose and temporarily immobilize the driver. We couldn't rap him on the noggin and leave him beside the road because we were descending into the subtropical area, where the villages were few and far between. There predators would take him quickly.

Dorothy stopped her yowling when she realized no one was paying any attention, and I drove in silence for another hour. Relaxing only when I saw that the deposed driver beside me had also slumped to sleep. Mostly I was conjecturing about Dr. Kalinga, and what was going to happen to him. He was intelligent enough, but with his weakness for the bottle, seemed a frail reed to support a reverse coup in Marundi.

For one thing, from what I heard, he had alienated all popular support there. But then I snapped fire under a small cigar, while driving with one hand, and grimaced at what I had heard. As a fringe brigand in such cases, all I ever heard was bazaar gossip and people rehearsing prepared convictions. Or hopes. Still, even if Kalinga had gone the way of Nkrumah and Obote, my agency wasn't spending a lot of time and money for nothing. He was useful to us, or potentially so.

For better or worse, Black Africa was closing to the

white man, and especially to the western white man. Among the things I had heard was that there were already over ten thousand mainland Chinese technicians at work in Tanzania. The weapon which killed popular Tom Mboya, heir-apparent in Kenya, was said to have been manufactured in Bulgaria. Kenya had already put all non-citizen merchants, for which read Indians, on short-term licenses. Nigeria had gone all the way; her government had barred all foreigners from small businesses, and a good many more not so small.

Soviet and mainland Chinese trade representatives were swarming over the emerging black African governments. A large U.S.S.R. display store in the heart of Nairobi's Kenyatta Avenue was showing Russian-built cars, tractors, industrial machines, and had impressive charts and posters on its functioning Ilyushin SST plane.

While I was raking through these random facts, another clicked in unbidden. I had read it in the *Ethiopian Herald* just before Kalinga made his impromptu ride. A day after my appointment at Lake Rudolph, with Dr. Kalinga in tow, Ungandan President Idi Amin and Sudanese Head-of-State General Gaafar al-Nimeiry were to meet in the Katangese capital, Lubumbashi, The Congo, and I wondered if General Pangolin would absent himself from the Organization of African Unity session in Addis Ababa to attend? . . . or if Marundi was important enough to be invited?

No answer came. I was shaken out of my reveries by a long giraffe ambling across the road before me. I had to brake suddenly, and swerve, to avoid hitting the towering beast. The giraffe seemed much less excited than I was, stretching his sixteen-foot height into a hitching lope only when the Toyota turned halfway around in the road. As I started down the road again, plowing through patches of mist, other game bolted in front of the Land-Cruiser. Tiny dik-dik antelope, peeping from the roadside, gazelle in

small flocks, with one lyre-horned male herding them, and
hyenas rocking away in their broken-backed gait, snarling
and grunting with their teeth bared.

As dawn lightened behind the dark mountain ramparts
to the east, I could make out flat-topped acacia groves. I
was beginning to react slowly, was nearly asleep, and
knew I ought to stop and let the Ethiopian driver take
over. But we were approaching Shashemane, the passing
point across the all-weather road we had deserted just outside Addis, and I did not trust myself to stay awake if I
put the military driver behind the wheel. So groggily I
slammed the lights of the Toyota off.

It was imperative that we get across the Shashemane
crossing and onto the dry-weather road west of it before
daylight. If we did not, our only option was to turn south
on the main road to Awassa, where another string of finance posts began. I was positive they had been alerted,
and that we would be collared unceremoniously if we had
to stop for one of them.

I rolled down my window, shook my head vigorously,
and with my right hand gave myself several stinging slaps
on the neck and cheeks. A hand came over my shoulder,
took the package of little cigars and the lighter from my
shirt pocket, and I heard the lighter snap. The hand came
back, and Maryam, the Danakil girl, put a lighted cigar
between my lips. I nodded and sucked on it, feeling more
awake; said, "Thank you" over my shoulder. The dark girl
did not reply, but I knew she had been awake all the time,
watching the back of my head.

I did not get full value from that cigar. Before it was
half gone, and I was rounding a corrugated curve, I heard
a distant thrashing and immediately turned the car off the
road and into a clump of banana trees. The Toyota's fenders chewed through the soft-fibred plants, and I socked the
vehicle into four-wheel drive and forced it further inside
the grove until we had only a latticed view of the sky.

The helicopter came angling down the road we had deserted, flying low. On its cab was painted the striped green, yellow, and red flag of the Imperial Ethiopian Air Force, and it would never have been that far down on the deck if it had not been doing reconnaissance. For us. I cut the motor, and leaning forward watched the whirlybird go on down the road toward Shashemane.

When I glanced around the interior of the Land-Cruiser, all of them were still sleeping except Maryam. *A tight ship we were running.* The Danakil girl smiled slightly at my expression of disgust, and I put a forefinger on my lips and touched it to her forehead. Getting out, I lost myself in the banana grove, relieved myself, and went to the edge of the descending road.

Below us lay the Rift Valley, that wide volcanic declivity which runs from the Dead Sea down across the Horn of Africa and into its equatorial hinterlands. We had already passed, in our night drive, four of its lakes below Addis, and I had a distant glimpse of Lake Awassa, to the southwest. My game plan was shot to hell; I had hoped we could pass the main highway in early light and hole up somewhere beyond, to sleep. With at least one helicopter combing the few roads, I knew that idea was a busted flush. We had to hole up now, quickly, and somewhere near.

To the right, on the descending roadway, a track branched off, leading back up the mountain escarpments we had been leaving. I could not see where the track led to, but it went winding upward toward one of the high Ambas, the steep-sided, flat-topped mountains which make our Arizona buttes look like anthills. The rough track didn't look like a tourist's outing, but I knew it was where we had to go. And stay, during the daylight hours, until we could try Shashemane crossing after dark.

When I got back to the Land-Cruiser, the rest of them were awake. Dorothy and Dr. Kalinga conversing by a front fender, which conversation he was punctuating by frequent sips of *tej,* Maryam stretching on the other side of the vehicle, and the Ethiopian driver having what seemed a troublesome bowel action, hunkered over at a decent remove of forty feet from the truck. However his head was obscured by the trunk of a banana plant, so no proprieties were offended.

We had more coffee, cold now, and Dr. Kalinga strengthened mine by the splashing of a little *tej*. And it did wake up the gut, no question about it. I explained about the patrolling helicopter, and said that we were going up a hillside track just beyond. To sleep until it was dark again. Nobody wanted any sandwiches, so we cranked up.

I drove up the mountainous track for half an hour, but could find no side standing. The Cruiser was in four-wheel drive all the way, and vegetation, including wicked wait-a-bit thorn bushes, clawed at the sides of the vehicle. Another indeterminate period of jolting and jouncing followed, and I saw that the Toyota was overheating, but was determined not to stop until I found a side stop screened from the track itself. The Amba loomed closer over us until it blocked out the rising sun.

I stopped, finally, because the remote and perilous track ran out. We were in a rocky clearing, facing the precipitous flank of the Amba. I was as surprised as the rest of them, and jerked the handbrake on. *Dead end, flat-topped mountain before our overheated radiator, no side roads . . .* Dorothy was hanging out the right-hand window, and she put the matter in perspective.

"Hey, man!" she shouted, "this is heavy. We've made the big scene, Shangri-La!"

The top of the windshield had cut me off inside, but when I looked upward I saw what she meant. The sheer flank of the cliff ahead ran up two hundred feet without a break. There was a natural rocky escarpment above, and on it, breaking the natural symmetry of the cliffside, a white stone gate with fluted sides. The top of the obviously man-made entrance was flat, and I wondered how it could be used. No goat alive could have made it up that vertical slope.

We were all out of the Cruiser, chattering and staring upward at this doorway into the remote mountain, when several men came out of the darkness of the high doorway to peer down at us. They did not greet us, wave, or offer any welcome. We stared up the vertical slope at them, and they stared back down at us. They wore shrouding white capes and conical white hats.

"We must bow to them," said Maryam quietly, from behind me. "They do not know why we have come, or what we want. And they can see we are not pilgrims."

"Pilgrims?" I asked.

"Yes. It is a monastery, hidden in the mountain. And unless you come as a pilgrim, you must have papers approved by the Bishop of Addis Ababa."

"So bow," I said, and we all went genuflecting solemnly. After another pause, a worn, plaited leather rope was tossed down from the shelf above. It was an inch thick, but posed another question. To Maryam I said, "you're the only one who speaks Amharic. Can you make it up to that ledge if I throw a seat hitch into the line?"

"No." Her answer was quick. "It is forbidden. No woman, no female animal, is ever allowed in such holy places."

"How about birds?" asked Dorothy, and I choked off a grin, reminding myself I had promised to dislike her. It seemed an impasse. I could go up the braided line hand-over-hand, but it wouldn't have helped much when I got up to the high gate.

"Perhaps I should have a go," suggested Dr. Kalinga.

"You speak Amharic?" I asked.

"Naturally, old boy. That and six other languages of ours, and five of yours, including Greek and Latin." The portly little black man walked forward, wrapped the big leather thong around one wrist, and went eeling up the line with perfect coordination. It was a splendid show, but unfortunately his strength gave out when he was only about thirty feet up. The *tej* had sapped him. Leaning out from the line, he bawled up at the faces peering down from the ledge, in fluent Amharic.

He must have shouted, "All right, chaps, a little help is indicated," because they began to draw him upward so smoothly that I thought there must be a windlass inside the cave entrance. There were a few minutes when everybody on the ledge was out of sight, and then Kalinga reappeared, to shout down at me.

"Sticky wicket here," he reported. "They say we are not pilgrims, and therefore must have the proper papers from Addis."

"Explain that we are weary tourists," I shouted back, "and that we would like food and shelter, a chance to sleep. For the privilege, we will donate five hundred Ethiopian dollars, in cash."

"That's the stuff to feed the troops," said Kilanga admiringly, and vanished from sight again. We waited. Dr. Kalinga came back to the ledge. "We've made a deal," he shouted, "if you send the money up first, tied to the line. But the ladies are not included. The Abbot says that this monastery was built in the ninth century, and no females have ever profaned it. He does not intend to break that precedent."

"Well, hell, Doctor," I roared back, "we can't just leave them down here, prey to wild animals and such."

"Not necessary. There's a footpath to the right. It leads to the next hill, which is not nearly so high. A nun who is apparently also a hermit lives at the bottom of a well to which she levitates on holy days, as I understand it. The ladies can use her hut."

"Okay," I bellowed hoarsely, and went forward to lash the Ethiopian money to the leather-plaited line. It went up swiftly, and a minute later Dr. Kalinga gave me the spread-fingered victory sign. I told the driver to go up, and he scrambled toward the ledge with his feet swinging free, no windlass action needed.

I took one of the loaded carbines out of the Land-Cruiser and led Maryam and Dorothy down the faintly discernible footpath around the base of the Amba. It led down into and across a rocky declivity, and soon we came to another, much lower plateau. On top of it were circling walls made of stones, in some places seven or eight feet high, and went through the maze until we found another cave-like entrance, this time with grassy vegetation growing on its flat roof.

We ducked inside, and found a long room with no windows. It smelled clean, however, and outside a cliffside door in the back we found a small spring splashing downward through the rocks. Still no sewer smell, and when I knelt to touch the water found it hot, almost scalding. Just below it was another circling rock fence, with stone steps leading down, going into shadow. Far below, we could see water moving, obviously from the same thermal source as the upper hot spring.

About forty feet down, jutting off the weathered stairs, was a ledge with a large dark hole behind it. I motioned Maryam Lalibela ahead of me, and she moved with easy grace down to the ledge. Dorothy and I were crouched several steps above her. Maryam called out softly, and an old, wrinkled woman wearing a white cape and the same white conical cap as the monks on the mountain above, put her body halfway out of the dark hole.

Maryam kissed her wrinkled hands and poured a stream of coins into them. The old nun-hermit had a protruding jaw and bucked teeth. She listened impassively to Maryam's request, nodded, and withdrew into her dark hole above the murmuring water, without comment.

"All right?" I asked, and the Danakil girl nodded. "Fine. You can at least have a hot scrub, and I'll see that food is sent down from the monastery." We walked back up the worn stone stairs of the well and into the low-ceilinged hut. I dropped the blankets on the floor, and handed Dorothy two bars of soap I had stolen from the Ghion Hotel.

She grabbed them and went sprinting toward the spring behind the stone hut, ripping off her blouse. I asked Maryam if she knew how to use the carbine, and she said yes. Then I told her that it was imperative that the Ethiopian driver not be with us when we went down the track toward the road, which would probably be at midnight, or before.

The Danakil girl nodded and went to her bag. She asked, kneeling beside it, how long I wanted the driver to sleep and I said a long time, ten hours, at least, and that I would arrange for his knocked-out keep with the monks, through Dr. Kalinga. She nodded, rummaged, and came toward me holding out two enormous blue capsules.

"They must be dissolved in fluid," she said. I took the capsules and thanked her.

With the cropped ringlets of dark hair, no makeup, and her ebony body seeming to burst out of the modest nurse's uniform, she looked like something from an ancient frieze, a Nubian courtesan having to put up with latter-day decadence. She even smelled like a woman, and I knew her black skin would be cool to the touch. Strange to think she had come meekly this far along the twentieth-century compromise trail, after her origin in the Eritrean desert.

"The man I talked to at the palace said you were Danakil."

Maryam smiled. "Do you wish to psychoanalyze me too? In the mission school, many *farengi* wished to probe the psyche of the Danakil savage. Then, of course, after we had discussed why the tribes of my people still lived by, and venerated, murder of their neighbors, they all wanted to see me do a native dance. Our tribal dances are jerky, and not very sexual. But most of them, in the interest of research, wanted to get their hands under my skirt."

I didn't answer, and the dark girl touched her right forefinger to her clean-cut lips. Then touched the finger to my forehead lightly.

"I could always stop that by telling them I caught syphilis on the Massawa waterfront, before I was twelve." Her English was precise, more American than British. "Do you too want your hand under my skirt?"

"Not unless you've got a certificate from your doctor," I said.

Maryam laughed out loud and clapped her slender black hands together. It was the first time I had heard her laugh.

"I will tell you," she said. "Although it is not very interesting. I remember a little about being a girl in the tribe. The men going off to raid neighboring tribes or ambush *farengi* caravans. Those who had killed a man within a year were allowed to wear a feather in their hair. Older warriors wore an amulet, ivory beads, or other talismen to proclaim the numbers they had killed.

"When I was eleven, I was sold to a slave caravan by my parents and taken in chains to Massawa. It was for less than you spend for a bottle of English whiskey, I expect. I was being loaded onto a dhow on the waterfront, with another girl and two Danakil boys, when I jumped into the water, scrambled up on another pier, and was being recaptured when Dr. and Mrs. Nichols, of the Seventh-Day Adventist Church, got the police to intervene.

"They were getting off a ship, going to join a mission of their church in Dessie, and they bought me from the dhow captain. I did not cost much, because they were taking me into Yemen. Black girls are no novelty there. The Nicholses made me a house servant at the Dessie mission, and were kind to me. She sat up many nights to help me get the School Certificate, and gave me books.

"The Mission at Dessie paid my way through the Empress Zauditu Nursing College in Addis, but I am paying them back out of my wages. There are not nearly enough trained nurses in Ethiopia, so now I can work all the time. It was a great honor to be chosen by the Palace to be assigned to Dr. Kalinga."

She stopped, and we heard Dorothy romp back in from her ablutions at the hot spring.

"Isn't it a fine thing that I was saved from being a desert savage?" asked Maryam.

"I'm not sure," I said.

"But you are sure about many things. You look at people and talk to them, but never really see them. You have decided. And you are always looking for an ambush. Everyone you meet is an ambush; you look through and around all people. If you were not a pale *farengi,* I would think you were a Danakil. Although that, too, is an invented name. My people call themselves *The Afar.* Why do you never wear the beads or talismen which tell of the people you have killed?"

I smiled, but not much. She was too close to the bone. "They aren't popular in my country. Goodnight, Maryam, sleep well."

I went hand-over-hand up the leather-plaited rope, and when I reached the ledge leading to the high gate was thankful that I didn't have to do it every day. Dr. Kalinga and the Abbot, who wore a flaring, loose robe, and a white cape, were waiting for me, and I bowed to him. The Abbott looked at least eighty years old, but his eyes, pouched in wrinkles, were clear, and his manner sprightly. He escorted us through the gate, along a rocky tunnel, and we emerged on top of the Amba. The monastery and chapel, weathered by eleven centuries of fierce seasonal rains and storms, were square, although most Ethiopian churches were round.

The outer walls of the ancient buildings were striped by alternate horizontal layers of stone and timber. Stone pillars supported the sagging doorways, and inside there was a nave and two aisles. The ceiling at the far end of the chapel had a paneled ceiling in good repair. In its squares, carved animals predominated. I could make out lions, eagles, and ibex, but a lot of them were gryphons and other legendary beasts. The windows of the buildings were sealed against the elements, but most of them had stylized carvings or plinths on the inside, and looked Byzantine in origin to me.

As we toured, Kalinga and the Abbot were chatting in Amharic. We continued through the monastery to its far end, went through another door, and approached the smaller buildings in the back, which housed the monks. They were much more crudely built than the monastery and chapel structures, and had high stone walls circling them to keep the constant winds off. We passed several water catchments cut deep into the Amba itself, and were shown to the large room allotted to us.

It was nearly empty of furniture, but had several rough

benches and handhewn stools. Our blankets, brought up from the Toyota, were tossed onto the straw which covered the hard earth floor. The long, low-ceilinged room smelled clean, even sterile. The Ethiopian driver was squatting in the far corner, ignoring us and dabbing what looked like coarse bread into a small bowl. The light was going fast, and I was about to drop in my tracks.

When a break came in the non-stop chat Kalinga was having with the Abbot, I said, "Doctor, tell him we are very grateful, but that we have come far and wish to depart at midnight."

"Not yet," said Kalinga in English, without looking at me. "They are bringing us food." And without missing a beat, he took up his talk with the Abbot again. I interrupted to ask where the facilities were, and he pointed to a small passage at the far end of the room. I went down it and found a ledge with footrests only, and two handholds carved into the stone sides of the passage.

It was a real adventure to have dysentery in that eyrie. Your tail hung out into space, and a steady draft of air blasted up the side of the mountain. Far below, another spring was gushing out of the rocks, which made admirable plumbing, but I had grave doubts about its safety for drinking. My gut was cramping, and I swallowed two Mexaform tablets dry.

When I returned to the sleeping chamber, several of the monks in conical caps were putting food on the benches, and oil-wick tapers gleamed fitfully from niches, blackening further the ancient smudges. When the repast was in place, we were poured *talla,* a spiced barley beer the monks brewed themselves, in horn-shaped containers. Then the Abbot, standing before his monks, made a little speech, and we bowed them all out.

The food tasted good, but then I was so hungry I would have attacked a live dog and spotted him the first bite. The unleavened spongy bread slabs were called *injera,* and you used them to mop, move, and lift the *wat,* which was a potent, pepper-spiced stew in a hot sauce. I knew as soon as the *wat* started scalding my taste buds that it wasn't going to help my dysentery a bit, because I had been through the same thing with chili peppers in Mexico. But that was a bonus yet to come; I kept mopping and eating.

Kalinga was grimacing, but kept going by having alternate shots of the homemade barley beer and Scotch. This, I thought in wonder, was probably the most far-our boilermaker known to any traveler since Marco Polo. I palmed the two large blue sedative capsules into my own horned beaker of *talla,* and had Claude add an inch of Scotch. After swirling the beaker a few times, and pretending to drink from it, I handed it to Kalinga and asked him to take it to the driver to say that we appreciated his help.

The driver was wolfing away at the monastery food when Kalinga approached. He looked up, squatting, heard of our gratitude, and drained the horned beaker. One problem solved. When I had set the alarm on my watch for midnight, I shook out a blanket and examined the straw under it. Then I lay down with leaden limbs. I was nearly asleep when Kalinga spoke again. He had paused halfway through another of his exotic boilermakers.

"Shall we stroll down to *le drugstore, mon ami?*" he asked pleasantly, "for a cognac?"

"Goodnight, Clyde," I said distantly, and was gone.

I awakened ten minutes before the alarm went off, which is something I have been able to do for a good many years. This was not my most happy emergence from sleep, however. Rain was slamming intermittent, solid blows at the monastery barracks, and a wild wind was whipping around the protective walls. *Another frigging worry.* If we made it across the Shasemane crossing on the main road south, our only routes would be along dry-weather roads.

The crude tapers had guttered out, but I could hear the driver bellowing with snores in the corner, and hoped that the *tej, talla,* Scotch, and sedative wouldn't stop his stout heart. When the soft alarm went off, I thumbed the knob and searched for my lighter. In its dim radiance, I saw Kalinga a few feet away, sleeping like a seraphic black baby, even to the fetal position. I got up, stretching, and leaned down to touch his shoulder.

He came awake immediately, and stared at my bending form. Perhaps, in the shadowed room, I reminded him of those enemies who had come to depose him, in the Marundian version of The Night of the Long Knives.

"Yes?" he asked quietly.

"Time to go."

He rolled over on his back and listened to the buffeting of the wind and rain outside. Then he heaved himself up, coughing, and started toward the narrow passage to the latrine. I gave him my lighter, and warned him about the precipitous ledge and the necessary handholds. He juggled the worn Zippo lighter, looking down at it, and asked why I had warned him.

"For Christ's sake," I said, "if you take a careless attitude out there you could fall on your ass, right into the bottom of the Rift. That's two thousand feet, bouncing off rocks."

"Thank you," he said, and ducked into the dark passage. I was puzzled, and I don't like to be in that condition. It suddenly occurred to me that the little black man might believe I had been ordered to assume his care and then arrange his death in some such remote place as this. It was a new concept, but then he had been rousted around considerably. Chased out without warning as his little country's chief executive, driven out of exile, shipped to apartheid South Africa, and now hurled into a wilderness in my care. . . .

When he returned, saying that the lighter had helped greatly but that he feared it would soon give out, I asked if he thought I had been assigned to kill him. He shrugged, and brushed at his rumpled jacket.

"I don't know," he said. "Noboby has explained anything to me."

I shook my head and followed the dying lighter toward the doorway. Dr. Kalinga hesitated, and asked about the driver. I said he would not be coming with us. That did not seem to reassure him.

"All right," he said, "but please do not call me Clyde again. It is not my name."

"This way, Doctor," I said, waiting at the door, and we both walked out and to the gap in the protective wall, hunched against the driving rain. Tapers were bending fitfully as we crossed back through the monastery proper and went down along the tunnel, to the high gatehouse. There were no monks present to see us off the ledge.

At a price higher than any Hilton suite, for only a few hours stay and some belly-busting hot sauce, it seemed to me that some of these Monophysite Christians could have lighted us out. Actually, the way down on the sodden leather rope, after I had locked the crude windlass, was not difficult. You could drop with ease, checking your fall with more assurance on the wet rope.

By the time I had opened the door of the Toyota, the lighter was guttering almost down and both Dr. Kalinga and I were drenched. I tried the motor, and it roared to life immediately. I switched it off, and had to go to the nun-hermit's hut on the lower hill almost by memory. That was a crock, too, and I fell heavily three times. Both Maryam and Dorothy were still sleeping. Fortunately, after I had stumbled over them and awakened the girls, Dorothy found that she had several folders of hotel matches, which I used while they dressed.

In another twenty minutes, holding hands while I led, we were back across the ridge and started down the overgrown track, with the rain blasting at us in sheets. Sometimes I lost the way, and the Land-Cruiser went bumping down the ruts until it lodged at a sharp turn. Once I had to break sharply, slam on the hand brake, and desert the truck while I eased the gut spasms caused by the hot *wat* sauce. That meant I lost another of the fine flax handkerchiefs which I order from Ulster two dozen at a time, and this fact made me illogically angry.

It took us two hours to make the road we had turned off when alerted by the Emperor's patrolling helicopter, and I heaved a sigh of thanks. But nothing improved; I started west in low gear but the slanting downpour was so heavy that the windshield wipers were useless. I feared they would get broken if I kept them going, so I switched them off and stopped.

In the few rain-driven glimpses I had of the road, I noted that its porous, red-earth shoulders were crumbling, being literally washed away down the ditches. So I switched the headlights off, and fumbled out a small cigar, hoping the tin had kept them dry. It had, but Dorothy's folder matches were soggy. I felt three of them fold limply, and threw the packet away.

We had nowhere to go, at least for awhile. Dawn was still several hours away, but the frigging rain was neutralizing our chances. We might as well not have ducked into the monastery. No one in the Land-Cruiser spoke, but I could hear them breathing all around me. I was aware that everytime Kalinga breathed, he was pouring highly flammable fumes around us all. And I didn't smell too good myself; a rain-drenched goat with his skin ripped in a few places, and the anger of adrenalin pumping an even more unpleasant odor inside the vehicle.

I tried to control my irritation by remembering all the hotel suites, fine food, and suppliant women I had encountered on easier contracts. It didn't work. I was jammed up, behind schedule, stalled in a bitching rain deluge that wasn't due for another month. *With a failed dictator, a half-savage nurse from the fiercest desert in Ethiopia, and a stupid, senseless little girl from my own country . . .*

The overhead light in the Toyota went on, and I said sharply, "Turn it off, please! That's all we need, to get stuck in this wilderness with a dead battery."

Ignoring me, Maryam Lalibela told Dr. Kalinga to move into the back seat. He did so at once. Then Maryam told me to slide over into the front-seat space he had been occupying. I did, and she came flashing over the seatback with long scissoring legs, holding her black bag. After a deft examination she started undressing me, first removing the rain-sodden jacket and short-sleeved shirt, and ordering me out of my trousers.

"Do you come as medical help, or short-term wife?" I asked, but she didn't answer. The soaked trousers were wrapped around my legs like leeches, and she helped me out of them. I had a bleeding right elbow, two abrasions, also bleeding, on the right side of the ribcage, and the ancient war wound on my left ankle had been torn wide open.

She cleansed them all, deftly, with alcohol-soaked swabs, and applied some kind of disinfectant I did not know, and I have been in a lot of hospitals. The stuff lanced pain through me, and I stiffened.

"Goddammit!" I cried.

"Hush," said the dark girl. The rain went on sheeting down.

AN hour before dawn the rainstorm abated and we crossed the main southern road at Shashemane unobserved. Our dirt road was fissured by the sudden rain, but if you stayed away from the shoulders there was no real danger on it. Rising sunlight filtered through patches of fog along tended rows of coffee trees as we drove on toward Soddo, passing scattered, conical huts.

Before noon we came in sight of Lake Abaya and began seeing beautiful little high-prowed fishing craft. Rolling through the wide valley hemmed in by blue ranges, we ate lunch. Bread, cold Danish sausages, Brie cheese, and mineral water. I was feeling better about our trek and thought we might make the Lake Rudolph appointment on time.

After passing the next lake, Shamo, we would turn due west for the final leg of our run to Lake Rudolph. That route was over another dry-weather road, but if it was as good as this one and we didn't hit torrential rains we should be able to average thirty miles an hour. In addition, the countryside was steadily becoming more subtropical, which meant more chances for concealment and few inhabited places.

I was counting these blessings when I heard the familiar clattering again and jerked the Land-Cruiser off the road immediately, and drove down a faintly marked lane between huge banana trees whose arching fronds shut out the sky. The Imperial helicopter must not have seen us because it racketed on down the road at about five hundred feet. We were still undetected, but it was now obvious that the palace in Addis Ababa had ordered a continuous square-search of all southern roads.

Dorothy started to speak, but I said, "Not now" and kept gunning the Toyota. When we were several miles off the road, I started looking for a place to shelter, saw another side road and turned down it.

That was a mistake. Without warning, the arching banana fronds over us ended and our vehicle was in a cleared area. At the far end of the clearing was a large thatched shed filled with people; several dusty Imperial Government cars were parked beside the structure. I rammed the Toyota into reverse and glanced at the rearview mirror.

Ethiopian soldiers had closed in behind us, so I switched off the ignition. The soldiers all had rifles and seemed to be wearing full field packs. Their topees were khaki, ornamented with what looked like tawny monkey fur, and the two officers wore black slacks with green stripes, green battle jackets, and their epaulets were flaring with the same monkey fur.

More soldiers came crowding out of the long shed, and behind them a wave of poorly dressed peasants. Dr. Kalinga started to say something, but I motioned him to silence with one hand. The soldiers behind the Toyota had not moved any further toward us, nor had they unslung the rifles.

"These people haven't gotten the word," I said quietly. "They're just curious. Maryam, get out of the truck with me and we'll walk into the palaver hall. The rest of you sit still and smile."

The Danakil girl swung out to join me and we went walking across the clearing. The Emperor's soldiers and the barefooted peasants parted to let us by. I nodded to them, but kept talking to the girl. Telling her that if the head man did not speak English, she was to tell him in Amharic that Dr. Kalinga and I were attending the meeting of the Organization of African Unity in Addis, as observers. That we and the American girl had been granted permission to make a sightseeing tour to Lake Rudolph and back. That Dr. Kalinga was not well, and she, Maryam, was accompanying him as a nurse.

"It is wise to use Dr. Kalinga's name?" she asked quietly.

"No choice. His name's on our papers. Anyway, I doubt if anyone here ever heard of him."

We went up the three crude steps and into the long shed. The only furniture inside was a crude table at the far end. A man was standing behind it, waiting for us. He was short, elderly, had an impressively big head, and wore a beard like the Emperor. His clothes were European, but of an ancient cut, and over his shoulders was an elaborate cape. To his left, sitting, was a black woman who had once been handsome but was now gone to fat.

She adjusted a white, embroidered *shamma* as we approached, and smiled coquettishly. One of her dark legs, surprising shapely, was thrust out, and a kneeling attendant was trying to extract something from her big toe.

"One of those bloody little jigger-fleas," she explained. "Quite painful, really."

Maryam and I bowed low, in concert, and the arrogant little man in the cape returned the bow. Straightening, he flourished his large, white-stranded fly whisk, and the corpulent black man standing behind him snapped his fingers and barked some orders. Barefooted servants came at us, jostling aside the peasantry. One carried a handmade chair, which he thrust under me from behind, and another placed a small and rickety table at my left elbow. More retainers hastily topped the table with lengths of vivid velvet cloths, a horned decanter, and a mug with a tapering neck.

Maryam received no attention at all. She still had her head down, and informed me that His Excellency was District Azmatch Makonnen, Dany (judge) of this portion of the King of King's realm. That he was pleased to receive such distinguished visitors. Would I present my official papers?

I handed them over and waited. Dysentery, bolstered by an increased adrenalin flow, prickled in my lower gut again. If the Azmatch noticed that we had skipped every finance post between Lake Abaya and Addis Ababa, the kaffeeklatsch might take a rude turn. But Makonnen was interested only in protocol. He flourished the papers back after a cursory inspection.

"Ask His Excellency," I instructed Maryam, "if he would add his signature. It would be a matter of great wonder to my countrymen, when I return to the United States." The dark girl repeated the request in Amharic, and Azmatch Makonnen gave an aristocratic shrug. Taking the papers back, he put his name at the bottom of every page with an American-made ballpoint pen, then banged away with two rubber stamps before him on the table.

I bowed low at the return of the enriched papers, and the fly whisk rotated again. One of the waiting servants sprang forward and filled two of the narrow-necked goblets with *tej*. A goblet was handed to the Azmatch, who tasted it briefly and spat out what he had taken. Then he hurled the vessel to the floor. The servants rushed forward and swept away the jug of *tej*. In a few minutes, while the entire company waited, they rushed back in and the Azmatch tasted the new batch.

This one was more to his liking. We raised our goblets to toast each other, and he was about to speak when his fat wife yowled and backhanded her primitive chiropodist ass-over-teakettle. His Excellency glanced at her with annoyance, and I asked Maryam to thank him for both of our kind reception and and his distinguished signature.

She started to speak, but he waved imperiously. "Go away," he instructed her. "I know English. In fact, I speak it perfect."

Maryam backed out of his presence, bowing, and the Azmatch and I had a touch of the *tej* together. After our second serving, I agreed with him. I hadn't tasted the first vintage of honey-mead, the one he had rejected, but this one was a real heart-walloper. I concluded that the Azmatch was the ideal man to take into Maxim's, in Paris; he was capable of cowing platoons of sneering waiters, and would have sent the wine back repeatedly if not satisfied.

His fat wife said something petulant, and the Azmatch flicked his whisk again. Another goblet was brought, and he poured her a drink. She sank back into her thronelike chair and sipped, bare feet clasped together. The Azmatch wanted to know about world conditions, and I told him they were terrible. Rolls-Royce had failed, the largest railroad in the United States had failed, the shipbuilders on the Upper Clyde had failed en masse . . .

This news seemed to cheer him immensely. He asked for more woe, but I said I would like him to meet my distinguished colleague, Dr. Claude Kalinga, O.B.E., graduate of Oxford and the London School of Economics, and an American girl who was touring with us. The fly whisk flashed again, and Claude, Dorothy, and Maryam entered the long shed. Kalinga, if no longer the glass of fashion, was still the accomplished diplomat, and he and the Azmatch struck it off immediately.

The girls, on being introduced, got only a curt nod from His Excellency, and a searching survey from the corpulent wife. A table was whisked in for Claude, covered with the same velvet swatches, and another decanter of the good *tej* was set on it. The girls were seated several paces behind us, got an unadorned table, and barley beer. They were not invited to join the conversation.

All these proceedings had been carried on with the peasants and soldiers crowding around us. The corpulent major-domo who always hovered behind the Azmatch I now perceived to be a eunuch. Whereas the official's wife had grown into her fat through an excess of good living, his was blubbery and of a neuter sex. The Azmatch several times roared away at peasants creeping forward, bending so low that their heads were almost on the worn plank floor. They were holding papers toward him.

He explained that these were petitions of various kinds, to redress wrongs in his other official role as a judge. The right of personal petition, he said, was as old as the Ethiopian Empire. And extended up to his Imperial Majesty, whose limousine was often halted in Addis by poor petitioners bolting out of the crowd . . .

Prompted by Dr. Kalinga, Azmatch Makonnen shook his oversized head in sorrow. The Empire had fallen on sad times. He could no longer have obvious malcontents shot by the roadside; this vitiated his authority. When he had been a younger Danya, he could hand over a convicted murder to the offended party's family, who could then take him home and torture him at will until they decided to execute him.

In the case of fraud, the debtor and the one owed were chained, or knotted together by their *shammas,* until the obligation was satisfied. Makonnen hastened to add that people of importance could hire surrogates to stand in their place for this intimate ordeal. I was fascinated by this direct form of punitive justice, and remembered a financial titan I had once known in Texas.

"The trouble is," he had explained to me, "that with all these stupid frigging laws nowadays, it's almost impossible to grind the faces of the poor anymore . . ."

The *tej* flowed on, and the afternoon waned. I don't know where they stored the explosive honey-mead, but it must have been a sizeable container. The Azmatch explained that he was only passing through this poor district on a semiannual tour. His headquarters were in Soddo. In late afternoon, the white fly-whisk flashed again, and court musicians appeared. Their leader was a capering dwarf, who sawed away with surprising virtuosity at the *masinko,* a one-stringed fiddle with a square sound box. He was backed up by a harpist whose instrument seemed to have come down unchanged from the time of King David, and another earnest player who kept his eyes tightly shut while thrashing around with a primitive tambourine.

I suggested, watching the sun's shadow lengthen in the doorway to this rough baronial court, that our time was limited and that we should be traveling on. The Azmatch was scornful; he said that we would feast soon, get to know each other better, and in the morning he and his men would see us on our way.

The *tej* kept coming.

BY the time dinner was over, it was nearly midnight. The *wat* (hot-spiced, peppered stew) and *injera* (spongy, unleavened bread waffles) were much better than they had been in the high monastery, but the Azmatch refused our compliments with scorn. In the good old days, he said, a feast meant drinking *tej* all day, then hauling in a fat cow and lashing it to the center-pole of the *tukul*.

When the celebrants were ready to eat, they used knives to hack steak off the living animal, and gulped them down raw. When they were ready to ball each other, they got off the benches and onto the floor. Not a prude or gourmet in the lot, apparently. I was prepared to believe this story of high living, but presumed they must have had very passive cattle or very stout center posts. Try that in West Texas, and after the first incision on a grown steer you would have considerable wreckage in your *tukul*.

Once again, I requested that we be allowed to proceed on our journey, stressing plane reservations in Addis. But the Azmatch was having none of that. His fat wife was hiccoughing gently and the belted chiropodist was back at her feet, trying to withdraw the elusive jigger-flea in near darkness. The shed was lighted only by flickering tapers.

"Now," announced the Azmatch, "I am going to show you something few Europeans have ever seen!" The musisians were dozing, but the Azmatch roared and kicked them back to life. The whole company surged out of the shed into full moonlight, laughing, shouting, and swinging depleted flagons of honey-mead.

Makonnen led the way up an incline at the back of the clearing. His big head was emphasized by the huge topee he wore; I didn't understand why he needed it under moonlight, but then there were quite a few things I didn't understand about rural Ethiopia. The Azmatch was fol-

lowed by his major-domo, the giant eunuch, and Dr.
Kalinga and I hurried to keep up with the stream of
comments Makannen was dropping over his shoulder.

Behind us came Dorothy and Maryam, and Mrs. Azmatch on a mule. An attendant ran beside each of her stir-
rups, which were bouncing around her extended feet. Behind the ladies came the reinvigorated musicians, the
shouting soldiers, and a considerable throng of local
drunks. We moved up to a hillside projection overlooking
the Rift Valley, surrounded on three sides by enormous
banana trees.

Like a mad professor on a tropical *Walpurgisnacht,*
Makonnen shouted back that the banana trees never fruit-
ed but were valued as food because of their roots. This
place was called Michichi.

The length of the grassy glade was broken by what
seemed jutting, slanting, fallen, and erect stone cylinders.
We paused to consider them in the bright moonlight while
the laughing company piled up behind us. All of the tapering cylinders were over five feet long, and the largest of
them towered to over twenty feet.

I had expected a stele, a jumble of ancient artifacts, or
at best a forgotten Coptic church.

What I was staring at was a forgotten priapic temple.
All these tapering stone cylinders, hundreds and hundreds
of them, were stone pricks. A tremendous gallery of erect
male members, every one loaded and ready to fire. All cir-
cumcized. For uncounted decades and centuries, they had
been aimed at heaven, enduring seasonal rains and storms,
ready to erupt.

Azmatch Makonnen had a torch; sweeping it around,
he led us through this ancient garden of fertility. His beam
played over spiderish hieroglyphics chiseled into the bases
of the enormous phalli, more than three feet thick.

Makonnen said that the origin of the male cylinders was
not known, but weren't they beautiful? The company had
crowded in around us, and Dorothy, directly across from

me, had both hands up by her cheeks. In wonder. As if to say, so this is where it's at! And all the time I was searching people in Joplin, Missouri. . . . Maryam Lalibela was smiling, as though she had known it all the time, and Dr. Kalinga was fingering this crotch like one who has been passed by when the artillery was distributed.

The phallic garden gave one pause. We were confronting the primal fact; the male member towering over me was three times as tall as I was. I reflected how high a man would stand, wearing *that* proud howitzer. *Some plead for the prophet's paradise to come, with gossamer-pantalooned houris undulating, but Michichi was the place...*

Men had long sought the Elephant's Graveyard and King Solomon's Mines. The Golden Fleece of Jason, and the fabled delights of The Old Man's Garden, where Assassins were trained. But this was the ultimate secret, the fierce and fecund heart of Africa, where all the unspent orgasms of the world were honored.

Bowing to the Azmatch, I said "Professor, we need a little mood music."

He flicked the whisk and instructed his giant eunuch. Lighted tapers were scattered on fallen members. The black dwarf sat astride a cylinder and began tuning his group up. More *tej* was poured, and the moonlit glade burst into life as the Ethiope combo pounded away. Dorothy went swarming up to perch on the point of an ancient circumcision, and the Azmatch's fat wife howled with laughter, straddling a lower projectile.

As the beat deepened, the revelers, intoxicated by *tej*, began cavorting around the glade. Maryam was watching me, which was proper, because I was watching Maryam. The Azmatch was laughing to see such revels; he threw his enormous helmet high in the air and began a strutting time step. Dr. Kalinga caught the big hat, reversed it, and began spanking out a Marundian drum motif to the Ethiopian players. The tempo quickened.

Dorothy dropped from her perch and ripped off her

shirt. Her young breasts quivered as she shed her skirt, shouting in unknown tongues, and went writhing through the ankle-deep grass. Someone handed me a horned goblet of *tej,* and I drained it and threw it aside. Kalinga left his topee-drum and began to circle prancing Dorothy, hands dangling at his sides, in perfect rhythm.

"Take it off, Claude!" she shouted.

I felt trapped in my clothes, and peeled out of my jacket and shirt. Dropped them at my feet, and bowed to swaying Maryam.

"May I have the next orgasm?" I asked politely, and her *shamma* and blouse were flung away. A sliding touch at her left hip, a flirt of the shapely legs, and the skirt was gone. Undulating toward me, the ebony beauty knelt and unlatched my belt, inducing in me the same priapic tension as the giant stones around us.

As I bore her down, the Azmatch and his wife cackled with laughter. It is not correct to say that I balled Maryam; instead I tried to control an explosion. With probing hands, lips, and her fine black body, she worked me out as no woman in my experience had ever done. Her frenzy was so savage that several times I wished I was wearing the Azmatch's helmet, because I couldn't tell where we were going to wind up. At one point, when I was briefly ascendant, I glimpsed Kalinga on his back with Dorothy impaled atop him.

When my vital fluids had been spent, I rolled over in the grass and shouted for some *tej*. Another beaker was brought me, and I had a belt of it. Maryam was watching me, squatted a few feet away.

"Was it good?" she asked, unsmiling. I kissed my index finger and touched it to her dark forehead, nodding.

The orgy in the phallic orchard was far from over. The beast with two backs was pumping everywhere, and a reporter from the *Kama Sutra* should have been there, taking notes. Even the black dwarf had put down his primitive instrument and was banging away at somebody, or something. Only the major-domo eunuch had escaped the crotch fever. He was leaning against one of the giant cylinders with a look of haughty ennui . . .

"I wish I had them all here," I muttered, finishing my drink. I felt eased, much like a male animal after a kill.

"Who?" asked the Azmatch.

"All the leaders of Women's Liberation. We could perch them on these stiff stone members and feed them *tej* until their nervous vapors dissolved . . ."

"Not much *tej* left," said the Azmatch worriedly. "Big party."

I laughed and, unbidden, climbed to a perilous stance atop the tallest of the rounded stone cannons. From that high perch, I favored those assembled with several choruses of "Where Has My Easy Rider Gone?", followed by a driving rendition of "Isn't Love A Gland Thing?".

Those in the audience who were not otherwise occupied applauded, and the ancient Ethiopian hills boomed back their approval. Under the unblinking African moon, almost hidden by the arching banana fronds, tiny dik-diks stood alert and motionless, astonished to see such frolic in the ancient meadow.

IT was a dew-bedraggled, *tej*-soaked group I roused at dawn the following morning. As we tiptoed out of the stone garden of Michichi, the Azmatch Makonnen, his fat wife, and the other revelers were still sleeping heavily. The black dwarf lay curled up with his head on the knee of the prostrate major-domo eunuch, and the musicians were sprawled among the other celebrants.

We went back down the path through the towering mock-banana trees, and as we passed the meeting-shed Dorothy Tyson suggested that we stop and make some coffee. I informed her curtly that we were already several hours behind schedule, and that if the Emperor's soldiers found us we would have years and years for making coffee, in an Ethiopian prison. Claude Kalinga looked rheumy-eyed but stoic; he had been to hangover-junction before. Only Maryam looked cool and unrumpled, but then she always did.

In half an hour, we were back on the main road to the southeast, rolling toward Arba Minich and Lake Shamo. As the Toyota cruiser gathered speed, Maryam lighted one of the small cigars and put it between my lips. I nodded thanks, glancing at her. The dark girl's smock was hardly creased, which was understandable because she hadn't had it on long after we entered Michichi. Nakedness, to her, was a more natural state anyway.

As she sat beside me, with her boyish, curling hair blowing in the morning breeze and her profile medallion-sharp, I thought of the legendary women warriors of Dahomey who had fought bare-breasted, in an elite corps of thousands, for the kings of that country. Armed with muskets and cutlasses, they had routed many male invaders.

The highway ran out at Arba Minich; after that there was only a track down to Kelam, the village which was our rendezvous point above Lake Rudolph. As we approached this junction, Maryam's head turned suddenly and she touched my elbow. This time, she had picked up the clattering before I had. I took the Toyota off the road into brush, and again one of the Imperial helicopters came low along the road, flourishing up a miniature dust storm.

We waited for half an hour, with the savannah heat invading the cruiser, and the 'copter swept back by us. That meant they had pyloned an Arba Minich and were on regular patrol. We backed out, continued southwest, and after two false turnoffs found the faint track to Kelam. Then it was bone-breaking time; the vehicle fought its way through wadis, across stony declivities and deep potholes. Soon all three passengers were hanging on as I fought the wheel; it was no accident that handgrips were installed in the rugged vehicle.

Some of the track was through grassy valleys where we saw more game than we had from the main roads. Wildebeests, antelope, and Grevy's zebra, with the narrower stripes. Once, just beyond a bamboo grove, we surprised three cheetah over a recent kill, and left them snarling but refusing to retreat. And occasionally we passed rude circular *tukuls* with small patches of tended ground next to them, but saw no natives.

At noon we stopped for lunch beside a small stream, and had a cold and unappetizing meal. When, in addition, I insisted on chlorinating the water, Dorothy yowled and spat it out and Claude did not even bother. From somewhere in the cruiser, he unearthed a depleted bottle of honey-mead he had salvaged from the orgy, and sat sipping it. Since the frigging water did taste terrible, I agreed with them. I had part of a cup and threw the remainder away.

As we bounced along the track, it grew hotter; we were rolling downhill toward the desert lands at the top of Kenya. The Northern Frontier District. Several times I heard springs crack, and felt the Cruiser shifting weight, but we had no time to wait or worry about that. Once we got bogged solidly in a swampy crossing fringed by papyrus grass and spent nearly an hour loading stones and brush under the wheels. Finally we came sucking out of the morass while I fed the Toyota full power, praying her four-wheel drive would not fail.

Although preoccupied with such vexations, I noticed that Dorothy seemed to be showing increased consideration for Claude Kalinga. The urbane little black man, far from being a burden, often lightened the tension by a wry comment, often adorning his words with poetical allusion. That was to be expected. But the girl from the white-supremacy Bible Belt of the United States was fussing over him, trying to make him comfortable.

Once, during one of these tender exchanges, Maryam handed me another lighted cigar, smiling slightly. So I had to suppose that Dr. Claude Kalinga might be packing around concealed penis power, and that it had come to light in the festive saturnalia at Michichi.

Just before dusk we stopped outside Kelam and concealed the Toyota in a bamboo grove. The place was not even a village, only a collection of scattered *tukuls* and a store, with a Norwegian missionary compound its principal feature. It did have, however, an emergency landing strip for light planes.

While we waited, Maryam walked down the dusty track toward the compound and the *tukuls*. The store had bloomed with lantern light, but most of the huts were dark. She came back in an hour with some tinned foods and juices, and reported that there were no government vehicles or troops in the place. That was good news. Although the palace in Addis Ababa had supposed us going toward Moyale, the main crossing point into Kenya, I had been afraid they would cover Kelam as a possible alternate.

We had a meal by the light of our own lantern, talking with the weary unconcern of four people who have been battered all day by what could not really be called a road.

Then the other three curled up in the cruiser's seats and went to sleep. I made an exterior check of the Toyota by flashlight, and saw that the shattered springs had sagged its fenders dangerously near the tires. It would not stand another such pounding.

I sat on one of the fenders, smoking and watching the faint lantern-lights in Kelam. Our rendezvous had been set for noon that day, but there had been no way to avoid the delay. Our frolic with the Azmatch had ruined the schedule. If I read the map properly, the emergency landing strip was about half a mile west of us, Lake Rudolph several miles to the south.

I was not sure the vehicle would make it to the lake, and hoped that those who were to rendezvous with us would come by air. Because in that place, we were nearly off the map. If we had to try for Lake Rudolph on foot, carrying supplies, and hoping to find boat transport, I would not have given much for our chances.

I was bone tired, and flaked out on the ground. But I could not make the blankets comfortable and lay a long time awake, staring at the stars. Finally I got up, and, probing with the flashlight, found Kalinga's bottle of honey-wine and slugged at it until I fell asleep.

I was awakened by the rising sun and heaved up from the tangled blankets. My three companions were still sleeping, and I strolled away from the vehicle to the edge of the mangrove-fringed swamp. And there, as an Australian friend of mine used to say, siphoned the python. Clouds of birds curvetted over me and wheeled back toward Lake Rudolph. A hook-beaked babou shrike planed down and settled in a flat-topped acacia tree, and I spotted a bare-throated thrush and a concal, strutting on the mud flat.

Several hundred yards away, almost invisible in the shade of the flat-topped acacia trees, I could see tall black, storklike members of the Turkana tribe watching me. Men and women, some of them with shoulder-slung piccanins, all motionless and watching.

Kalinga came to stand beside me, and as he yawned and urinated, asked if I knew where we were headed. And for what reason?

"No, Claude," I answered, "I am being staged along, the same as you. I was ordered to Durban to escort you to Addis Ababa, then to this rendezvous. We were supposed to be here yesterday at noon, but I'm sure someone will contact us today. They know the kind of country we had to come across."

"All right." The little black man nodded; he looked dispirited and his London-cut clothes were rumpled and smelly. "I'm only a counter, and probably a lesser one, in the business. With my present future, anything would be an improvement. However, I would not like to be bartered to Pangolin, just as a sacrifice."

I didn't answer, only watched the shrike glaring down at us as Kalinga buttoned up his fly.

"I realize," he continued quietly, "that you think I am a drunken, blithering oaf. A man would have to be that to

89

do what I did in Addis when I was a guest of Selassie. But I was not always such a fool, you see. My lineage goes back in an unbroken line to Nzinga a Nkuwa, of the Congo Kingdoms. Twenty-two generations of paramount chiefs."

The shrike flew away. "I wish you luck, Dr. Kalinga," I said.

"Oh, hell . . ." He smiled wearily. "Just call me Clyde. As you said before, it's a type."

We walked back to the Toyota, found the girls awake but not enthusiastic, and were brewing coffee over a small fire of eucalyptus twigs when we heard a faint droning. I kicked the fire apart, stamping its embers. The cruiser was already parked under trees, so we did not have to worry about its being seen from the air.

A single-engined plane came out of the sun to the southeast and made a direct approach, buzzing the emergency strip. It must have been clear of livestock, because the pilot booted the plane around in a steep bank and put it down like a leaf. I went to the edge of the mangrove swamp and stared across at it. Kenya registration, only the pilot inside. He jumped lightly to the ground and started taking off his gloves, glancing around.

I told Claude to cover me with one of the rifles, and went skirting around the swamp toward the airstrip. The pilot was a stumpy, swarthy man of middle age; he nodded as I approached, and checked the number of the passport I held out against a note from his jacket pocket. Holding out his hand, he said he was Ernie Vukovic, on charter out of Nairobi, and where was the rest of my party?

I pointed toward the eucalyptus grove, and Vukovic said I had better fetch them. He was running late. That he had been on the strip yesterday at noon, and had waited until four, but there were no lights so he couldn't wait. We were to bring only clothes and toilet articles, no weapons, food, or anything else.

"Where are we off to?" I asked.

"Keekorok Lodge, in the Masai Mara Game Preserve."

"After that?"

"After that I don't know. I leave you there and go back to Nairobi. So collect your people. But burn everything personal, eh?"

"Right." I went trudging back toward the eucalyptus grove. The mounting sun was beginning to be a blow, and we were all sweating before we had emptied the truck and burned what we did not wish to take. Claude delayed us, searching for something, and finally admitted he was looking for the rest of his bottle of *tej*. When I admitted I had belted it away, he shook his head mournfully.

"One blow after another," he murmured, and we walked to the airstrip with our meager baggage. The plane was not built for five people, but Vokuvic, a cigar stub between his teeth, powered her off without difficulty. In a little over an hour, flying at about a thousand feet, we were circling a lush oasis in the bush. Towering shade trees, green lawns and several large log cottages around a central building and filling station. The air strip at Keekorok was lighted and paved, so I knew it must be on the main safari route.

After we had landed and unloaded, several native boys in dark trousers and white sports shirts grabbed our baggage and headed for the nearest two cottages. Someone had already registered for us. Vukovic began supervising the fueling of his little plane, and when I thanked him, he winked and nodded.

Maryam and Dorothy were put into the nearest cottage, and Claude and I were quartered in the one just beyond it. There was a swimming pool in the center of the manicured lawn, and monkeys swarmed up and down the tall trees. Beyond this luxury row, I could see a large mud-walled native compound, but it was in the bush. Everything outside the main lodge and the luxury bungalows fringing the tended lawn was in the bush. Someone had spent a ton of money to carve out this oasis.

I looked inside Claude's bedroom and asked if he was all right. Since he had the room boy cornered, and was ordering a double Scotch, he assured me that things were marching well. The two bedrooms had private baths, and were air-conditioned. I walked to mine, unlocked it, and found a man lounging in the big chair beside the desk. He was frogfaced, half-bald, in shorts and a bush jacket; familiar too.

"Hello, Joe," he said, reaching to shake hands. "Paul Snyder, from the Embassy in Nairobi." I nodded; we had worked together in Karachi once. Lifting the carafe on the desk, I had a drink of the chilled water, and told Paul it was nice to see him again. It wasn't, because between us we had screwed things up good on the Karachi assignment.

"So what have we got?" I asked.

"You're going on safari tomorrow, into Tanzania. To Seronera Lodge, in the middle of the Serengeti Plain. Leave at nine; there's a white Silver Spear cruiser ready, with a driver named John Mikumi."

"We're just on safari, hunh, like rich people?" I asked.

"Right. Until you get to Seronera. Only Dr. Kalinga won't be one of the rich people. He's hot as a pistol. So he'll wear black pants, a white shirt, and sit beside the driver, going as a servant, you understand."

Snyder unzipped his brief case and handed me a sheaf of papers. The top one was an official license for a game-parks guide in Kenya and Tanzania and had Kalinga's picture on it, but the name was George Matabele.

"So he'll be just plain George to the rest of you," warned Snyder. "Tell your people that if they forget it, they can get him killed in a hurry."

I leafed through the other documents. Another U.S. passport and international certificate of vaccination for me, in another name. I handed Snyder the ones I was holding, and he put them into his brief case. A Kenyan passport for Maryam Lalibela, who was also somebody else, but just as handsome in the picture. Dorothy's new passport was made out to a Helen MacKenzie, but bore no picture.

"Had no time, man," said Snyder. "I'll fake it with a Polaroid black-and-white."

The other papers were health certificates, Tanzanian visas, and Kenyan reentry permits. Snyder suggested that I check them over for flaws while he went next door to grab a head shot of Dorothy. The papers and documents were in order, so far as I could tell, and in a few minutes he was back with an American-Gothic portrait of Dorothy. While I watched, he trimmed it with a razorblade, went out to get an iron from the maid, and with a damp towel pressed it into the phony passport.

Then he handed me a leather wallet filled with U.S., Kenyan, and Tanzanian currencies, ten thousand dollars worth in all, and I signed a receipt for it. We checked the papers over again.

"Okay," I said finally. "This gets us to Seronera. What's after that?"

"Man!" Snyder rolled his eyes and lifted his hands in supplication. "I just check you through my territory. It has taken me three days and nights to get this stuff together, and my love life has suffered. All I want now is to see the ass-end of you and your little group."

He did look beat, so I suggested that we order a drink. Snyder said he could have only one because Vukovic was waiting to fly him back to Nairobi. While we had it, he said that Dr. Kalinga's wild ride on the Emperor's horse and my flight with the American girl, after assaulting a member of the Ethiopian upper classes, had caused considerable diplomatic static, and that Neal Pearsall was angry as hell because both State and his superiors were chewing on him.

"Tough shit," I commented. I was tired, and had sweated so much I was afraid to lift my arms for fear I would faint. Snyder knocked the last of his drink down and said that the whole thing seemed fairly well screwed-up, but that the blackbird, Maryam, was a beaut.

"Dr. Kalinga's nurse," I explained. "And I never mix business with pleasure."

"Rooster's ass, comrade. It is to laugh." Good old Paul Snyder shook hands again and went striding across the smooth expanse of lawn, followed by a troop of chattering monkeys. In a few minutes, I heard the light plane snarl off for Nairobi.

THAT night Dorothy, Maryam, and I had dinner in the main lodge. Kalinga got only a tray in his room, but didn't seem to mind. I had explained our next stage to him, and he was working on a quart of Scotch when I left him. The dining room was ornate, imitation Hilton and nearly as bad, and in the lowering twilight we watched a huge bonfire being set aflame beyond the glass wall. Hidden spotlights illuminated the water hole at the far edge of the western lawn.

While we were having coffee and brandy, two bull elephants came lumbering into the lighted pool, the smaller of them trumpeting and squealing, to roll in the red mud. Buffalo with flat, twisted horns came to the edge of the light, but no further. Marabou storks hitched along the banks of the pool, and the elephants there lashed their trunks at them angrily. They retreated a certain distance, watching. Lions coughed and roared outside the perimeter of the floodlighted water hole, but we couldn't see any of them.

While Dorothy squealed and Maryam smiled, I damned myself for a cynic but could not help thinking that the same animals, precisely the same animals, would be back for tomorrow night's show. And why not? The water hole was protected, food was provided, and there were always the tourists to look at, behind the glass wall.

When we walked back to the bungalows, I told the girls goodnight and cautioned them against recognizing Dr. Kalinga as anything but plain old George. A game-parks guide, duly licensed. Otherwise, as Snyder had stressed, it might suddenly become dangerous for him. When I looked into his room to say goodnight, I found that Claude was still being dangerous to himself. He had fallen asleep in a chair, in his clothes, and his food was untouched.

In my own room, I showered again and was toweling when I started sneezing. That was the air conditioning. *Jesus,* I thought, *you can't win,* and shut off the frigid air and opened the windows to the warm air of the African night.

In the morning, as before, Claude had breakfast in his room and we went to the dining room. We were wearing the new safari clothes Snyder had brought from Nairobi, and they fitted well. We were inescapably branded as tourists; even Maryam looked like a handsome Negro schoolteacher from the States who had blown her savings on the trip. John Mikumi, the Toyota driver, was a handsome young black man who bowed and helped the room boys load our new finery. Claude was slumped in the front seat; his bloodshot eyes seemed to say that he considered the whole effort as a farce.

We drove for two hours on a good dirt road, passing many giraffe and one herd of about sixty elephant before we came to the striped pole of the Tanzanian border station. There, as the languid black soldiers pawed through every case slowly, I realized why we had been cautioned to bring along nothing of our original personal effects. Our passport numbers were checked against a list held by a suspicious lieutenant.

It was a tight, nervous border. I had known, from common gossip, that the East African Federation of Kenya, Tanzania, and Uganda was falling apart. Obote's overthrow, Amin's fear that he would try a return coup, and Nyrere's obvious support of the exiled Obote, had everybody nervous. The only stable factor was the old M'zee, Jomo Kenyatta, President of Kenya. When he was gone, the only statesman in the black African states, the Federation would go up in flames. If it lasted that long.

Finally we were waved through, after as severe a shakedown as I had seen in years of enduring them, and rolled on toward the Serengeti. For the next few hours we saw many giraffe and zebra, small herds of antelope, and flee-ing warthogs with their tails hoisted, but not much else. When I asked John, the Wakamba driver, if this was really the fabled plain which held a million wild animals, the handsome black boy smiled at me over his shoulder.

"Wait," he said.

I waited for another two hours, until late afternoon. Then, without warning, we were engulfed by an endless sea of hartebeest and wildebeest, interspersed with zebra, antelope, and slinking hyenas. The spotted scavengers were circling the herds, waiting to seize the newly dropped antelope young. I had been told in Addis that when the herds were on the move, unless the calves could rise and and follow the procession in only a few minutes, they would be ripped apart by the carnivores.

These herds staggered the imagination; they covered the roadway and filled the flat horizons of the Serengeti Plain in every direction. Because neither humans nor domestic animals could live with the dreaded tsetse fly, this was the last great domain of the wilderness animals, who were not affected by the fly. Their numbers, filling the whole plain for miles, could not be contained by the eye. As John moved the cruiser slowly through them, the ungainly ante-lopes bucked and shied aside. The white Toyota plowed a slow furrow through a sea of grazing animals.

"This, sir," said John, over his shoulder, "is the princi-pal herd of the Serengeti on its eastern migration. We are fortunate; we have caught them surrounding Seronera. In another day, they will have passed on."

"How many animals, John?"

"I do not know, sir. I am told that there are usually a quarter of a million in this principal herd."

It was easy to believe. We went on plowing through them for another ten miles, in low gear, before we saw Seronera Lodge ahead. And even as we rolled into the grove of high trees and rocky escarpments, the grazing animals were all around us. Seronera was a dusty sorry sight, even with the last sunlight draining off it and lamps blooming in the rondavel windows.

The customs hut was closed, and the small museum opposite it. This seemed odd, because Snyder had told me that Tanzanian authorities checked every safari coming through, no matter what the time. The reception hut of the lodge was also closed, but after we had climbed out to stretch I went into the small bar next to the shed-type dining room and located a black man in the kitchen. He got keys from somewhere, and led us to two shabbily thatched, ancient rondavels. Beyond them stretched a lane of green tents, all dark.

In the lengthening twilight, we followed the man I had cornered in the kitchen. He unlocked two of the dilapidated rondavels, which stunk with the stale perfume of insecticide endlessly applied. All around us; before, behind, and ahead, hyraxes were leaping and bounding along the dusty paths. They were like oversized guinea pigs, furry athletes dropping from the rocky escarpment, the water tower, and leaping from one rondavel to another.

My concern was that on this main stop along the East African game-parks route, we had seen only one person, a black servant so badly frightened that I could smell it. With shaking hands, he unlocked the first rondavel door and switched on the weak light, then motioned Dorothy and Maryam inside. Then we followed him to the next conical hut.

When we were standing inside it, I turned to the black boy and asked sharply if he would bring our baggage along. He nodded.

"And dinner. Can we get food?"

He nodded so vigorously I thought his head would come off. When I tried to tip him, he dropped the key on the floor and fled out the door.

Kalinga sat on one of the iron beds, lighting a cigarette.

"Claude," I said, "we're in trouble."

"I know." He flipped the match away, his head down. "This place is the second stage for safaris. From here to Ngorongoro Crater, Manyara, Amboseli, and Tsavo. But there are no white men here."

Outside, in the tropic night, hunting lions grunted as they circled the herds packed around Seronera. A hyrax thumped through a hole in the dusty thatch above us, and burrowed into a nest above our weak, unshaded bulb. What I was thinking of, mostly, was that we didn't even have a peach-tree switch to defend ourselves with.

"Claude," I said hesitantly, "I was briefed in Keekorok. This stage of our journey was planned. By my people, and they would not knowingly send us into an ambush. Now I'm going over to that bar and get us a bottle, some ice, if they have it, and some soda water. Okay?

"Certainly," he said, but did not look up. I didn't blame him, because I knew that he was thinking that he was in too deep; that he had trusted too many people, including me. I turned toward the door, but didn't make it to the bar. I didn't even make it outside. Feet were tramping in unison, and when I reached for the door knob it twisted in my hand and I was forced back.

The man who came in was tall. Under a gold-visored garrison cap, he had a flattened nose and protuberant lips. Almost no neck; his square jaw ran down to wide shoulders accentuated by comic-opera epaulets. So gaudy that he had to be either a field marshal or a doorman at a *luxe* French hotel. The broad planes of his face, under the pop eyes, gave him the same armored look as his namesake.

The automatic pistol was on us, and the intruder was smiling with sardonic satisfaction. I knew who he was, because I had memorized a lengthy file of pictures on him. *Dock worker, failed boxer, bodyguard for politicians in Marundi, an officer's commission bought through planned murders. . . .* Finally, a general officer and Defense Minister under Kalinga.

General Pangolin, who had broadcast an offer all over Africa. *One million shillings for the return of deposed President Kalinga alive, one East African pound for his carcass. . . .*

While we stood under the gun, there were more trampings in the dusty lane outside. Our rondavels were being surrounded, and all the lights in the Seronera Lodge flashed on. Claude Kalinga gave our visitor a tired smile.

"Hello, Leonhor," he said. "Did you come to kill me, or to collect your own reward?"

THE bounding hyraxes sent up dust spurts as we were escorted from the rondavels to the center circle of Seronera's compound. The place still seemed deserted and the feet of the shuffling soldiers behind us sounded loud along the path. From outside the brooding grove of trees came bellowings, coughings, and the hyenas' harsh laughter as they circled the nearby herds. There were lights in the lodge buildings, the bar-dining shed, and the rondavels.

Kalinga and I were walking behind General Pangolin. I looked at the back of the black general's big head, with the ornate garrison cap set too squarely on it, and thought that Pangolin represented the inevitable second stage for the new governments of Africa. First, logically, had been the natural leaders among the blacks, the few foreign-trained intellectuals. Men like Nkrumah, Obote, and Kalinga. Two of the best, like Tom Mboya, and Patrice Lumumba had been casually slaughtered. Of these primary leaders, only the M'zee, Jomo Kenyatta of Kenya, had developed into a statesman and patient father to his people.

The others had invariably progressed to a megalomania which led them to shortcutting democratic processes, corruption, and even building statues to themselves. They had a right to fail, of course, even as early white leaders had failed. Or to lose impetus or direction, as had Banda of Malawi, when he sought an accommodation with South Africa's apartheid.

In failing, they left the door open for the thugs and butchers like Pangolin.

In the dusty circle before the bar entrance, two men were kneeling, their hands steel-cuffed behind them. Multicolored radiance from the string of lights over the bar terrace fell across their bowed heads, and put colored stains on the drooping white trumpets of the moonflower bush behind them. The flowers wafted out a sweetish mortuary aroma into the tropic night.

We four prisoners were halted, and General Pangolin and his aide stepped forward onto the dusty circle. At a harsh order from Pangolin, the aide seized both kneeling men by the hair and jerked their heads up. Twisting them to face us. Even though the dark faces were contorted, I could recognize the two security guards who had been with Kalinga in Durban.

General Pangolin shot them both through the back of the head, at close range. Considerable greyish matter pumped suddenly from the frontal exit of his bullets, followed by bloody fluid. When the aide released their hair, the two executed men pitched forward quivering and died with their faces in the dust.

Pangolin was watching us. He had not changed expression, and the machine pistol was hanging at his side.

"You," he said conversationally, pointing the pistol at me, "will get the same treatment tomorrow morning. Dr. Kalinga, on the other hand, will be going home with me. A welcoming ceremony has been laid on in Sokoto."

I remained silent, because the blood-lust was on Marundi's latest dictator and I thought he might handle my case offhand, if given any provocation. Kalinga was not so diffident.

"You were always stupid, Leonhor," he said quietly, and he had never sounded more British or condescending. "It would be a great mistake even for a violent cretin like you to kill this man. He is employed by the United States of America, and is acting under orders. His murder would cause an immediate cutting-off of aid funds from that country."

General Pangolin laughed. "The fellow is just one more of their secret agents. They would not even admit he was missing. And as for the miserable trickle of American aid their Congress has just cut it all off. Everywhere."

The musical-comedy epaulets buckled as his heavy

shoulders turned; he was grinning at someone off to his left. I followed his glance to four men standing there. They were Chinese, dressed in dark western suits, but held themselves like soldiers.

"His government would ranson him, Leonhor," insisted Kalinga. Pangolin considered this possibility briefly, thick lips pursed.

"No time for messages. We have to leave here by midnight. I've had all the safari roads blocked for forty hours, waiting for you, by radioing that bridges were washed out. By tomorrow both Nairobi and Dar es Salaam will be sending troops to see why the tourist trips are stacked up." He motioned irritably to his aide and turned toward the bar.

The aide was ordering soldiers to escort us back to the rondavels when Kalinga called out again. Curtly, as if he, not Pangolin, was in charge.

"Leonhor!"

"Yes," Pangolin turned. Rage was beginning to buckle his broad black face.

"Let him go, and the girls. Safe cond ct back to Keekorok. Then I will discuss the Lausanne matter with you."

Pangolin's clouding face smoothed out. He snapped some orders in Marundian, and Claude was escorted into the bar with him, under the string of garish colored lights. Dorothy, Maryam, and I were taken back to the second rondavel, and locked inside it. That was a joke, that lock. I could beat it in one minute, with a coathanger.

Sentries were posted on both sides of the door, and another at the back, although there was no back door. A hyrax thumped down on the conical thatch roof, and stared down at me through a large hole. His beady black eyes glistened in the faint reflection from the bare bulb. Dorothy and Maryam went into the bathroom to take turns under the tepid shower, and I sat on the edge of the hard iron bed and listened to their muted talk but not really hearing it.

I was considering the position. It was not promising, but as Samuel Johnson said, nothing so concentrates the mind as the prospect of imminent death.

DOROTHY must have showered first, because she came back into the bedroom while the shower was still running. Naked except for a towel around her hips, her hair matted and glistening, her firm young breasts pointed at me like nippled eyes. No urgency sparked my loins; so far as I was concerned it would have been just like screwing an open grave.

Snyder, my associate, had intimated in Keekorok, that I was a man who would frig a snake. And I believe that this was a general impression in the agency, but entirely unfounded. I have never seen a snake toward which I had amorous inclinations, even if the technical problems could be solved. Dorothy, for me, had about the same attraction.

"What will they do to us?" she asked, freeing the towel to dry her hair. That was so insolent a provocation that under other circumstances I might have low-bridged her, just as a lesson.

"Nothing, I hope, to you and Maryam. So far as they know, your papers are in order. But unless Claude makes some kind of a deal, Pangolin might shoot me."

Dorothy stopped toweling her hair, saddened. Then resumed her task.

"Do you think?" she enquired earnestly, "it would be safe to brush my teeth in this rusty tap water?"

I stared at her. *So much for affairs of state.* And assured her that she might die a lingering death if she used the tap water, even for a douche. Got the thermos jug off the table, handed it to her, told her to quit pointing her tits at me and get out of sight. She pouted and switched back into the bathroom.

Maryam came out, decently, if not fully, clothed, with her dark ringlets damp. She looked cool and imperious. Her ebony elbow looked more desirable to me than all of

Dorothy's nakedness, and when I got up from the bed she
retreated, laughing. So I told her that in about an hour we,
she and I, were going to break out of the rondavel.
Through a hole I would make in the back wall, while
Dorothy created a diversion at the front door, which I
would unlock from the inside.

As always, she went to the heart of the matter. "Won't I
slow you down?"

I put my hand back of her slender neck and kissed her
generous mouth, soap-tasting from the shower. "Probably,
Nefertiti. But we'll have to strike across the bush, and my
Swahili is nonexistent."

Her head went back; she was smiling with more radiance than I had ever seen on her face. "Am I really like
her?"

"How long, Egypt, how long?" And I was kissing her
again, from the hips up, when Dorothy came back out of
the bathroom. She said "Well!" and went to work on her
straw-colored hair again.

"My Swahili is not fluent," Maryam warned, but I assured her it was good enough. To Dorothy, I explained
that after I had chopped an exit hole in the rear wall of the
rotting rondavel, she was to start screaming and run out
the front door. This chore, on first consideration struck
her as dangerous, and I assured her it was. That she might
get shot, or raped, but that it would create enough confu-
sion to let Maryam and I escape from the compound. That
such a diversion might save my life, Maryam's, and con-
ceivably her own and Claude's.

I think the mention of Claude's safety brought her over.
She rehearsed my instructions several times, and said she
was ready. Watching her, I thought, *all her life she's been
a walk-on from Joplin, Missouri, a face in the crowd. Now
she has something important to do, and will probably
make it big.* I was not discounting the possibility that she
would be shot down by a trigger-happy sentry. Or, if she

didn't make enough noise when she stormed out, to be a bitch-dog for all the nearby soldiers.

Getting through the back wall of the ancient rondavel was like chopping through butter. I was using the rocker-arm I had broken off the antique water-closet, and the only problem was to keep from opening the hole outside prematurely. Maryam was kneeling behind me, piling the dislodged straw-and-baked-mud material under the bed. When the hole was ready, I unlocked the front door and stationed Dorothy before it.

By this time, she was beginning to understand what was involved. And whispered tremulously to me, asking what she should be screaming. Anything, I said; the Boy Scout oath would do, but pitch it high and frantic. Then I knelt beside the hole, with Maryam crouching beside me. Asked her if she was ready. When she nodded, I knocked out the last half inch of the hole and went eeling through it.

As I did, Dorothy turned it on like an air-raid warning siren, flung open the front door, and went dashing out. Her soprano decibels knifed at my ears as I broke out of the hole with the iron rocker-arm. The sentry at the back had not deserted his post, but was turned away, to check the sudden altercation. I turned him slightly, by one shoulder, and the curved iron flail broke his thorax and neck. He slumped, dying as he fell.

Wheeling back to the jagged hole streaming weak light, I whispered to Maryam and she came crawling out to join me. I had the sentry's rifle and the extra ammo from his belt. Skirting the high rock outcroppings at the edge of the compound, we left Seronera in the shadows. Behind us, loud American rock music and drunken laughter were coming from the bar.

Our solitary passage was disturbed by a massive shadow among the acacia trees, and I brought the rifle to port and snapped its safety off. A giraffe went undulating away in sections, almost noiselessly, to vanish among the taller eucalyptus trees. Hunting lions were near the dusty road we skirted, and a troop of wedge-headed baboons crossed the road, barking angrily. For them, I waited, putting a hand behind to stop Maryam.

A mile from the Seronera compound, there was a fork in the roads. A sickle moon was riding high, often obscured by broken clouds, and the arrowed, fading signposts read NGORONGORO CRATER to the south and MASAI MARA KEEKOROK to the east. We turned east, and many times had to shout at the grazing wild beasts in order to go ahead. The animals were unafraid of us, and had to be startled to break up their masses.

As we went along, I kept listening for sounds of pursuit, vehicles from Seronera. None came, so I hoped that Claude Kalinga and General Pangolin had something constructive to talk about. I was also worrying about Dorothy Tyson. When they found the dead sentry, and equated it with our hole in the rondavel wall, she would be in trouble. But we could not stop.

After we had walked five or six miles from the road junction, Maryam said she had to stop a minute. While she retreated behind some wait-a-bit thorn bushes I lighted one of the last of my little cheroots. When she came out to join me again, we stepped back out on the dirt road in time to see a caravan of vehicles approaching. My first thought was that somebody had sprung the safaris from the Kenya side before Pangolin was ready.

Snatching Maryam's arm, I dragged her back into the bush, hoping that the high-beam headlights of the approaching caravan had not picked us up. My hope died when spotlights mounted on the first vehicle flared on and began to sweep the road. That meant they were not safari cars. Hustling Maryam deeper into the bush, making her run, I lunged for some kind of sanctuary.

PULLING Maryam by the hand, I bulled into the Serengeti bush. We followed the flashlight's beam through sparse, thorny vegetation, often stumbling on the uneven ground. This terrain had never been plowed, and except for the scant grazing it gave the gaunt Masai cattle herds and the migrating ruminants, would never be touched until the tsetse fly was conquered.

After a hustling quarter-mile, in which our clothes and skins were slashed frequently, I knew we had to go to ground. When I stopped, Maryam dropped to her knees, panting. Staring through the dark night, I looked for any refuge; a cluster of trees, a dry wadi, even a marshy pond where we could hide in the papyrus grass.

Off to the right my glance was checked by a low, rounded silhouette. Dragging Maryam back to her feet, I struck out for it. As we got closer, the rounded silhouette took shape; we could smell a fire burning and smell cattle dung. Two hundred yards away, we stopped again. From that distance, we could make out the oblong compound surrounded by a thorn *boma*. That was the protective thorny hedge surrounding the temporary village. Inside was a row of rounded huts not more than four feet high; inside the huts a corral where cattle moved. Fitful moonlight glinting on their horns. And although we could not make them out, goats were there, too. One of them blatted out a hoarse call.

I whispered to the girl that the place was a Masai *manyatta*, one of the migrants' temporary homes. And cautioning her to walk behind me, I approached the thorny *boma* and circled, trying to find a break in it. I knew the entrance would be closed against marauding animals, but we had to get inside and there was only one way in. The stench increased by quantum leaps as we got nearer.

109

When I saw what appeared to be a double thickness of the *boma*, I flipped the flashlight on again. The moment I did, there was a near whisper by my head, and a seven-foot metal-tipped spear thudded into the nearest hut and hung there quivering. The spear had been thrown from behind me, and I wheeled.

"*Jambo,* goddammit!" I shouted. "Let's be a little care-full with those things."

As the flashlight beam swung across the brush behind us, branches were pawed aside and a tall Masai warrior stepped out. He was tall, indolent-looking, and held another metal-tipped spear ready. I knew very well that if he had wanted me, the first one would have been planted in my back. Or Maryam's. She had been directly behind me.

The Masai did not speak. He wore a faded orange robe, and his hair was coated with a mixture of ochre, mud, and cattle dung. Although the spear was still ready, he was stooping slightly. Waiting for an explanation of why we had approached his habitation under cover of darkness. Dark eyes set in the finely chiseled Nilotic face were curious, but not disturbed.

"Tell him in Swahili," I instructed Maryam, "we are friends who need sanctuary quickly. Enemies who mean to kill us will come soon." The Danakil girl murmured that her Swahili was more Amharic than Kenyan, but that she would try. While she was speaking to the tall warrior, he remained impassive, watching first me and then Maryam. While she was pleading with him, there was no sound from within the darkened huts, although there must have been twenty of them. There was only the sound of penned cattle moving, and occasionally lowing, and goats bawling.

The warrior let her speak for what seemed a long time, but was probably only a couple of minutes. Then, without changing expression, he lowered the spear. Put the butt of it on the ground, and stooping still more, hooked his right foot and ankle around the grounded shaft. It was an odd but unmistakable movement of relaxation.

"Mamma," he enquired in English, "will you drink milk?"

Maryam bowed to him, whispering that it was a traditional greeting. I knew that the Masai drank the blood of their cattle, but for such famous warriors to offer milk to visitors seemed strange.

"Am I included?" I asked. "Or does only mamma get milk?"

"You, of course, too," the warrior said. "I will hide you and feed you. I not only speak English, but I own an English Leyland truck."

"Can't beat that," I admitted, and he raised his voice sharply. In a tongue that was not Swahili, the *lingua franca* of East Africa, which had allowed the Danakil girl from Eritrea's deserts to talk to him.

Masai families, more warriors, wives, and children began to press around us, pouring through the opened *boma* gate at this command. Several of them carried oil lanterns which had been bought from some *duka-wallah's* store. And as soon as the light fell across them, clusters of flies began to hum around their nostrils, ears, and eyes. The warrior who had flung the warning spear at me had not been troubled by them, so perhaps it was the flickering smoke from the lanterns.

The warrior led us into the interior of the *manyatta,* which turned into a stinking quagmire under foot. As we went along, both men and women were probing and pawing at Maryam and myself. The flies buzzing around their faces seemed not to bother them, except that they kept one hand free to fan at them while frisking the visitors with undisguised curiosity.

I had to duck low as we were escorted into the chief's hut, and wondered why a race whose men were well over six feet tall should build habitations they could not stand up in. I didn't worry about it long, however, because the stench inside the *manyatta* hut was so overpowering that the outside assault on the nose seemed like a fine French perfume. We were offered a bowl of discolored milk, which I presumed had been mixed with cattle blood, and I gagged some down.

Maryam seemed to have less trouble with it; perhaps in her childhood in the Danakil desert, they had offered her a similar ration. We were seated together on the packed earth floor, and the warrior who had ambushed us earlier was talking to Maryam, again in Swahili, when he suddenly pushed up from his crouch. One finger went up in warning, he seized the spear which had been canted over his shoulder, and ducked back out of the low hut doorway.

The Masai women left with us extinguished the smoking lamp, and through the doorway we could see the dim lights going out in the other huts across the central corral Maryam took my hand and I felt her trembling. She had never done that before, not in all our vicissitudes since leaving Addis Ababa. I put my arm around her shoulders.

She whispered that the reason many of the Masai children, even the backslung babies, had fresh cicatrices cut into their cheeks and at the outer edges of their eyes was to draw the clotting of flies to fresh blood, away from the eyes themselves.

The Masai *manyatta* was silent. The moon had broken through the overcast, and we could see poor cattle milling around slowly, their hooves slopping into the mud. The goats, too, and several small donkeys. I knew that the warrior who had met us, together with his other *moran* warriors, was outside in the brush, waiting with spears poised. Then, long after they had heard it, I picked up the hum of moving vehicles coming closer. They were being driven in four-wheel drive, crunching through the low brush, wheels spurning the sparse grass on the sandy soil.

I stood up suddenly and struck my head against the mud-wattled roof. My impulse had been to hustle out and find the Masai chief, to warn him he must not throw a spear against men holding rifles and rapid-fire weapons. But even if I could find him, standing alert and storklike in the bush outside the *manyatta,* I could not tell him. In the darkness, there was no chance to haul Maryam along with me.

I have often been called a sonafabitch, and never deny the justice of the title. But I did not want to see the people of this *manyatta* wiped out by Pangolin's men, after they had given us sanctuary.

The vehicles outside were moving in shorter bursts of engine power, and I knew they were ringing the *boma*-enclosed huts. They were positioning themselves; we could hear their transmission cases and differentials dragging across the brush. One after another, the motor sounds were silenced, and the searchlights began probing across the backs of gaunt cattle.

Stepping outside, I vaulted up on the top of the low hut, holding both arms high in the ar.

"No shooting, for Christ's sake!" I shouted. "No shooting! We will surrender."

Several of the searchlights mounted on the vehicles swung to pin me in their radiance. The roof of the hut was buckling under my feet, and I nearly lost my balance, but kept both arms aloft and kept bawling, "No shooting!"

Silence hung over the *manyatta.* I struggled to keep my balance on the yielding hut roof, the Masai huddled in the dark below, and the only sound was from the penned livestock. The cattle had been spooked, and were milling and bawling in the small corral.

"Come out," came a shout from behind the bright spotlights, "with your hands held high."

I nodded vigorously, turned and jumped down from the buckling hut roof. When I called Maryam, she came out immediately. We went back through the stinking mud to the *boma* entrance. As we walked toward the nearest vehicle, the spotlights on the others swung toward us. Our arms were up as high as we could get them.

Men began to move past the lights toward us. They were not uniformed; all wore the same cut of khaki shorts and bush jacket, and carried sidearms and cradled carbines. As we approached the vehicle, I saw it was a plate-armored military vehicle, with a full-traverse heavy machine-gun snouting through the front slit.

A beefy man waiting beside the vehicle ordered Maryam and me inside it. As we crawled past the first seat into the windowless interior, he jammed his carbine into my back so hard that I stumbled and fell to the metal floor. Then he prodded me in the tail with the muzzle of the weapon, laughing. I clawed my way upright and followed Maryam into the back, bleeding at both elbows.

Two soldiers were lounging on the narrow seat on the far side of the armored car. They watched with detached interest as Maryam and I took the metal-rail seat on the other side. The only illumination came from a shaded light set over the passage to the front seat. The bulky soldier who had jammed and prodded me with his carbine swung into the front seat and gave a curt order.

The spotlights snapped off, motors roared to life, and in orderly precision the fleet of armored cars began to withdraw from around the Masai encampment. At a glancing, rough-caught count, I had made them at least ten vehicles, perhaps two more. In compound gear, snarling across the lateritic soil and sparse bushes, they converged back toward the highway.

When we reached the road, the armored caravan turned east. One of the soldiers lounging opposite us leaned across and offered me a package of Gauloise cigarettes. I took two, nodding thanks and not fearing cancer because no self-respecting carcinogen would associate with a cigarette that bad. When he flicked a butane DuPont lighter, I sucked them both to flame and handed one to Maryam.

As we rolled eastward, away from Seronera, I reflected that the interesting thing about our captors was that they were all white men, and handled their weapons with easy competence. They did not have insignia of any kind.

WE rode inside the armored car for a little short of forty minutes, by the count I was making, but I was unable to determine our direction except that we had started east after leaving the *manyatta*. The interior of the vehicle was windowless at our level, although there were firing ports slitted beside swiveled machine guns above our heads. The interior of the car grew smoky and stifling, and the two men lounging opposite Maryam and myself watched us with amused dispassion. Up ahead, at the right side of the narrow companionway. I could see half of the bulky, thick-necked mercenary who had prodded me so playfully with his carbine.

The last ten or eleven minutes of our ride was rougher, and I knew we had turned off the main safari road. When the heavy vehicle stopped, we were ordered out. As I stepped to the ground, Maryam was holding my left hand, and the blocky mercenary chopped the barrel of his weapon down across our grasp. It hurt like hell; Maryam winced and put a bleeding hand to her mouth, but without making any sound. I was getting a trifle vexed with this unknown warrior. I have no objection to force, *per se*, but it ought to have some object.

With my own hand stinging, I looked around the blaze of lights in which were were centered. The place was a small natural amphitheatre set in a circle of the rocky escarpments which dot the Serengeti Plain, and the only entrance into it was a narrow gorge through which more cars of the armored column were still pouring, and parking neatly and discharging the bush-jacketed white men who wore no insignia. The enclosed space was such a natural fortress that no invader short of strafing or bombing aircraft could have damaged it.

The entire south and west walls of the inner side were

covered by cantilevered tiers of glass, stone, and steel, four stories high. The lighting was indirect and the total prospect oddly pleasing. Frank Lloyd Wright would not have disowned the skill which had made it fit the site. Huge trees passed at intervals all the way up through the building, but were separate from it, protected by glass-sided shafts which left their trunks open to the weather and their top foliage bending in the night wind.

Muted colors sparked on all its levels; wall mosaics, fountains, and rough-textured rugs. So skillfully had it been done that they concealed the bleakness of the steel and glass, which only framed the serene candelabra and massive, hand-hewn furniture. Over the lintel of the wide stairway marching up to the first floor was a carved sign which read WOLF HOUSE.

After the shabby comforts of Seronera Lodge, this fantastic structure hidden among the rock-rimmed hills seemed like an African Shangri-La. Strangest of all, although it must have had a hundred balconied rooms, in addition to the huge dining room and two bars I could see from where I stood, it seemed deserted. An unoccupied and extremely fine oasis dropped into the Serengeti.

The blocky mercenary ordered us up the stairs, and started to swing the cautioning carbine again but I pushed the muzzle of it aside. Without haste, because the copper-salts were salivating into my mouth.

"Don't prod us with that thing again, friend," I advised him. "We'll take the order. Don't overdo it."

His square face hardened. *A pig, a bloodlust man, with pale eyes and straw-colored hair*. He pointed up the stairs with the snout of his carbine, and we mounted it. He followed. Below us in the courtyard of Wolf House, the bush-jacketed troopers were lounging against their cars, talking idly and firing up smokes.

As we walked by the large dining room, I saw that a log fire was blazing at the far end, beyond a sea of dark-red napered tables holding formal dining settings. But nobody was seated at the tables, and no waiters were in sight. The place was like an elaborate stage set done in faultless decor, but the cast had not shown up. As we paced by, with the mercenary's paratrooper boots thumping behind us, I noticed that the bar, built into a rock crevice, was also glass-sided, a huge curved pane that had been cut to conform to the arc of the rock and seemed to have grown out of it.

The next two floors were equally luxurious, but all the rooms seemed to be small suites, because I saw no other public rooms. On the fourth landing, we emerged from the shaded hallway onto an open terrace fanning off a rock ledge. To the right, a small waterfall fell down worn rock paths into a natural pool. This open area near the top of the escarpment had an unobstructed view, in every direction but east, over the endless stretch of plain.

This side of the waterfall was another, smaller bar set into a declivity of stone. As below, the lighting was so unobtrusive that I thought the open plateau probably could not be seen at all from the level ground several hundred feet below. This level, unlike the lower floors, was populated. A red-jacketed barman was on duty, and he was white, too. Sitting at a table near the edge of the high terrace were two men.

One of them I had seen before: in Korea and Biafra, although he had fought in many other places since serving Hitler in War Two. Indochina, the Middle East, and Algeria had also known him. He was the other mercenary leader, a slender man with a scarred, suntanned face. He was holding a drink below his sharp chin, watching us approach.

His companion was an enormous man wearing a tasseled tarboosh on what seemed a completely bald head; even without it, or the tan tropical suit of tussah silk, he would have automatically invoked a whiff of the Levant. He was not watching us; his massive face was bent toward a tripod-held Quasar nightscope. He was sweeping the dark plain below him. I knew what the heavy-barreled scope would do, what its tremendous definition was, because I had long coveted one. But they come high; the type he was working went for thousands, not hundreds, of dollars.

At a warning guttural from the cretin behind us, we had stopped and were waiting. The fat man did not lean back from his scope.

"A pleasure, Mr. Gall. And you, *Madama*. Have seats, please."

His tone was not entirely Beirut, Cario, or anything placeable. It was the total Middle-East inflection of the *souks*. The mercenary pointed out a chair to Maryam, the one beside his silent associate, and gestured to another for me. Beside the fat man bent to his observations. Instead of taking it, I reached for another one and was twisting it around, to straddle, when he cursed and jabbed me in the back again, savagely, with the muzzle of the carbine.

Screaming with pain, I fell forward, putting both hands behind my back. When I hit the stone floor, my right foot was hooking behind his legs and I rolled across his fall. Pushing halfway up with the other foot, I snatched the carbine from his hands, relaxing to meet the drop, and pushed up, reversing the weapon. I chopped him once across the broad jaw with its butt, felt the bone crack, and dropped it for a double-handed smash into the groin.

He jackknifed suddenly; it was his screaming time. He writhed on the floor, clutching his testicles and bawling hoarsely. I had again reversed the carbine, and had its safety off. The slender mercenary had not moved from his relaxed position, although he wore a shoulder-scabbarded machine pistol. The fat man sighed, and sat up straight. He rubbed at the massive deltoid muscles seeming to anchor his huge head.

"Impetuous, Mr. Gall. They told me you were quite sudden."

"He kept poking me with this frigging thing," I said.

"No manners." And put the carbine down on the table beside the fat man. The soldier with the locked, ascetic face had gone kneeling beside his anguished comrade, and was probing at his jawline with tanned hands.

"Mandible's broken," he announced, trying to steady the twitching, contorted body. "Balls smashed, too, but we ought to get the jaw set." Reaching into his jacket pocket, he pulled out a plastic kit, removed a needled syrette, and snapped off its point. Pumping out a drop of the colorless fluid deftly, he pinched a fold of skin in the writhing man's upper arm and stabbed him with the point.

The hurt man slowly stopped jerking, and his howls throttled down to a moan. Looking up at me over his quietening body, the older mercenary said quietly, "Try that with me sometime."

"You never know," I replied, and uprighted the chair I had originally chosen, then turned and straddled it. During all this exchange, Maryam had been sitting with her knees together, watching me. The fat man had been leaning forward, pudgy, manicured hands steepled under his chin. He handed the intact mercenary a thick wad of shilling notes.

"He's a fool. Put him in a car for Keekorok. We'll radio ahead to have him airlifted to Nairobi, and get a hospital bed for him there, so the thick-headed Afrikaaner can get patched up to let another man break his jaw."

The kneeling mercenary nodded and said something in German to the barman, who had not moved during the altercation. In a few minutes, two of the troopers came down the shadowed hallway and took the limp man away. The thin soldier followed them down the stairs, and I heard him giving crisp orders in the courtyard below. A vehicle hummed to life and roared out through the narrow opening, its passage racketing off the stone ledges.

The fat man listened to the sounds of departure, then shook his head and turned his bulk toward Maryam. "You must *perdonome, Madama.* I am not a good host, but we are under some pressure here . . ." His massive arms flourished, as though he would be mute without their free exercise. "I should have arisen when you came, isn't it so, but my bulk is so great I cannot shift it idly. But we are glad you brought Mr. Gall. You will have to drink?"

She had tea, and for us he ordered double J&B Scotches. While we were working on them, he said that the man I had hurt was Klaus Brecht, a stupid South African, and that the real leader of his troops was Rolf Trenkel. I nodded, sipping my drink without relish. I had been wound up so tight that it took several slugs at it to break up the tension in my stomach.

I didn't need any information about Trenkel. He was, in the limited sphere of men who make their living by violence, a top-drawer celebrity. He had been, in World War Two, a corps commander in tanks under Guderian. When the dream of a Third Reich which would last a thousand years had guttered out in a Berlin bunker, he had escaped to Spain. Joined the French Foreign Legion, and been in at Dien Bien Phu. A cool and resourceful officer, he had next turned up in Katanga, as Moise Tshombe's chief of staff. He may have there supervised Lumumba's execution. Biafra saw him next, and for a brief few months he looked like winning. . . .

No dice. He was taken off in a light plane flown by the Swedish pilot, and was said to have nursed that defeat in Capetown. When the revolt in southern Sudan erupted, there he was again, a skilled organizer and deployer of their guerrilla forces. By now a legendary, hired leader of lost causes. That effort was no different, and he fled to Kampala for sanctuary. Was arrested there, sitting in full view at an outside table of a sidewalk cafe. Flown back to Khartoum, under an automatic death sentence, he was suddenly released from prison, probably for information given when the three-day coup against al-Nimeiry collapsed.

"Interesting," I said. "Now may we know your name?

And why you have gone to such great expense to get me here?"

"Oh, sir!" The pudgy hands arabesqued. "I have as many names as you. In Lebanon, I will be one name, in Istanbul another. I think that if you call me Aristide Valeuris, in our present business, it will be enough."

"Fair," I said. "What is our present business?"

Steepling his hands under his third chin again, Mr. Valeuris began to tell me about it.

MR. Valeuris was as pontifical as an updated Sidney Greenstreet of the bazaars, and he put considerable body-English into his phrasing. The alerting word was in the second sentence he pronounced, and the correct word sequence followed in the next sentence. This was the man, the one I had been instructed to meet for the delivery of Dr. Claude Kalinga. Which meant, in theory, that the rendezvous had been made.

A grievous flaw was present, however. I no longer had possession of the deposed Marundian dictator. General Pangolin had relieved me of the prize. I pointed this out to Mr. Valeuris, but he arabesqued his meaty hands, said that this was obvious and as much his fault as mine. Would I hear him out, and did I wish him to speak without restraint before Miss Lalibela?

"Yes," I answered, to both queries. And before he could crank up again, asked how he had known my name.

"Sir, you are too modest. A star, even a constellation, in your own line, whose works have long been noted. Besides that, I sat for two hours watching you in October of 1968. The Haji Terrace Bar, in Damascus." He shrugged like an elephant primping. "I was far too insignificant to warrant your attention, of course, because I was playing chess on a corner of the bar."

I stared at Maryam, not seeing her; my mind was going back to 1968. The fat bastard was right. I had been in that bar, in Damascus, at that time. And I did not remember him, which was like overlooking the Leaning Tower of Pisa. Plus the fact that even if he had seen me there, that fact would not have given him my right name. I had been drinking with a cultural attache from our embassy in that bar, so M. Valeuris seemed to be well-connected.

He flourished out a card, expensively engraved, which

said that Aristide Valeuris of Beirut, Lebanon, was an ac-
credited representative of the Anglo-African Development
Trust. No street or cable address, or telephone number.
Valeuris seemed to be a man who contacted people, instead of the other way round.

"Sounds grand," I admitted, "but I am not familiar with
the firm. Therefore, to me, it could be no more than having such expensive cards printed. Your office, for example,
might be in the sky, or beyond the Mountains of the
Moon."

I felt perfectly safe insulting Mr. Valeuris, because he
was so obviously a rogue. In addition, he came with the
proper credentials; we could speak straight out to each
other. He rumbled with elephantine mirth.

"Oh, sir, we are of far more substance than that, I as-
sure you. If I tell you once the names of our principal in-
vestors, will you and the *Madama* here then forget them?"
When I nodded, he dropped the corporate hammers on us.
"Rio Colorado, The Antelope Trust, Anoa Copper, Griz-
zard Freres, Vega Hermanos S.A., and the Oriente Energy
Group."

I shrugged acceptance, since the combined assets of
these corporate bodies ran into billions of dollars and indicated a consortium of mining and petroleum giants which
had a record of rearranging small governments in the past.
In the past decade, however, they had been forced out of
their South and Central American holdings, and were
being threatened in many other places around the world.

Valeuris amplified. Most of the emerging black nations
in Africa had enough mineral resources or tourist possibil-
ities to give them a viable economy, "even though the
bloody Kaffirs haven't brains enough to operate a wheel-
barrow, without foreign advisers." Marundi was one of the
few poverty-stricken states which had literally nothing to
attract foreign investment. It remained a poor, mud-hut
cousin to its more affluent neighbors.

This had changed six months before Dr. Kalinga was

deposed. A London geological survey team had discovered enormous deposits of wolfram in the bleak Kildin Mountains. Did I know what wolfram was?

"Tungsten," I said. "Valuable in producing high-alloy steels."

Valeuris nodded. The Anglo-African consortium he represented had signed binding contracts with Dr. Kalinga as sole concessionaire of the rich wolfram find. He, himself, he announced with great sadness, looking like an aggrieved quarter-ton baby, had supervised the signature of these documents in Sokoto, capital of Marundi. The necessary heavy equipment, procurement of managerial and engineering personnel, and an enormous fleet of lorries and river ore boats had been contracted for and were en route to Marundi when Dr. Kalinga was unceremoniously chased across the border at midnight.

To compound the injury, he added, a sum of pounds sterling in six figures had been placed to Dr. Kalinga's advantage in a numbered Swiss account, in Lausanne. That name jerked me sharply back to Seronera, and Kalinga's offer to Pangolin, his last-ditch counter. His willingness to discuss "Lausanne."

"So you see, Mr. Gall," said Valeuris, "that the situation was not at all tenable. Besides the expensive private bribe to Dr. Kalinga, the consortium had committed itself to the expenditure of millions of pounds to put its operation in train. Then this gangster, General Pangolin, declares the deal off and is currently negotiating with the People's Republic of China to develop the wolfram deposits. Can you not see, sir, what a blow this is to our western economy?"

I could see it very clearly. Under the terms Valeuris had indicated, Marundi, having no bargaining leverage, was to have been the victim of one of the most tremendous steals of modern times.

"At this point," he continued, "I was instructed to avert the folly. There was only one way to do it; restore Dr.

Kalinga to power. He could then honor the contracts previously signed. That is why you were assigned to bring him to me. I was to meet you in Seronera, but certain difficulties made me a day late. That was time enough for Pangolin to bring troops in ahead of us, and snatch the good Doctor.

"So the problem is simple. We must get him back and restore him to power in Sokoto. Fortunately, we have the means to do that."

"Wait!" I semaphored my hands before the torrent of confident words pouring out of the fat man. Colonel Rolf Trenkel, the slender mercenary, had come up the stairs to the outside terrace, and sat with one booted leg hooked over a bar stool. He regarded me without expression, like a starving hawk.

"I want to fit a few things together," I continued. "It appears that you have invaded the Serengeti Plains with a considerable force of hired soldiers under the command of Colonel Trenkel. With the money at your disposal, that is not unique. The fact that this corps of mercenaries is riding in an armored column does seem unusual. I have just come from Seronera where General Pangolin had another small army of invaders and promised to execute me in the morning.

"I did not see his transport, but I presume that it is at least as adequate as yours. The main safari routes have been blocked, thus denying a major source of revenue to Kenya, Tanzania, and Uganda. I am not a political expert on black African governments, but you don't have to be that to know that President Nyerere of Tanzania would never allow two such forces to invade his country. Not without screaming to the United Nations and world opinion."

Valeuris smiled and fired up a twisted cheroot big enough to be a cane for a dwarf. "Sir, you simplify. Julius Nyerere is in Dar es Salaam. We are on the Serengeti. All Pangolin had to do was skirt around Lake Victoria with his people; the frontier there is guarded by a few corporals. And you are wrong about his transport; it cannot compare with ours."

"Unhunh. And how did you infiltrate a couple of hundred white, trained soldiers into Tanzania, a black nation?"

"Anybody can go on safari, Mr. Gall. We brought our men in from Nairobi, Kampala, Dar es Salaam, and Arusha, in small groups."

"Driving armored cars?"

Mr. Valeuris rumbled again with laughter. "No, sir. That was later, once we were all inside. Simplicity, sir. Simplicity, itself. The Tanzanian Army was on maneuvers, far from the capital. A rather large outlay of cash convinced the commanders in the field that they should spend three days on strictly infantry training. So we took over their vehicles, and left them in bivouac."

I whistled at the thought of what that must have cost. Colonel Trenkel was still brooding on his bar stool, like an elongated El Greco duke, and I decided to punch him up a bit.

"Okay. I'm not sure I understand all I've heard, but you have a force in being. Here, now. Ready to operate. And the leader of this force is Colonel Trenkel. A good soldier, certainly, but the most consistent loser the world ever saw. He lost under Hitler, he lost under Tshombe in Katanga, he lost in Biafra, and he barely escaped being executed in Sudan. What makes you think he can be a winner now?"

Valeuris' wide mouth tightened, discolored teeth clamped on the twisted cigar and lips clearing the gum line. He glanced toward the solitary figure lounging on the bar stool. Rolf Trenkel seemed not to notice it; he was sipping at his mineral water, but I knew he would kill me if he could do it without cutting off his paycheck. That was what I counted on, his paycheck. He had been a fine soldier once, but for over two decades his life had been directed toward killing people for money.

When Valeuris spoke again, his voice was softer, and a little hoarse. "I always get the best man I can. That was why I had my principals request your services. And Colonel Trenkel is a distinguished soldier, especially on this type of operation."

"Agreed. But I repeat: he has never had a winner in his life."

Rolf Trenkel put his glass on the bar, and went down the wide stairway.

"You have offended him," said Valeuris. "Was it necessary?"

"Probably not."

Valeuris wiped shreds of tobacco from his mouth. "I implore you to forget these old hatreds. In a couple of hours you and Colonel Trenkel will lead a ten-man commando team into Seronera, to reclaim Dr. Kalinga. Then our armored column will drive into Sokoto and put him back in power."

"In daylight? Through those herds of antelope, a quarter-million of them?"

"Yes, Mr. Gall. And as your forthright President, Mr. Truman said, 'If you can't stand the heat, you must get out of the kitchen.'"

I stood up and stretched. "Okay. Where is our room?"

Mr. Valeuris turned and motioned to the bartender. He came out and escorted us down the stairs to a double room. Maryam went into the bathroom to shower, and, fearing she would not soap herself well enough, I joined her. Lathering her perfect black body was a great pleasure. When we were both clean, we got into the single beds separately and she reached across to clasp my hand.

I flipped the lights off with my other hand.

"I am your woman," she said quietly, "for as long as you want me. Please do not get yourself killed."

"Never do that, princess," I said. "I'll be gone before you wake up, but not for long."

WHEN the soldier came down the dark hall to fetch me, I followed him without awakening Maryam. Rolf Trenkel and the other eight mercenary officers were grouped around a table in the sumptuous dining room, but it was dark except for one lamp over their heads. Colonel Trenkel was leaning on the table with both arms spread; a map was between them. He looked old and tired; his flaxen hair was thinning. His eyes were pouched in shadow.

"You will lead the four men on that side of the table," he said in Teutonic-inflected English. "Because my Number Two is taking his food with a straw and you broke his balls."

The other soldiers of fortune stared at me with bleak eyes.

"We have two hours and a few minutes until dawn," Trenkel went on, "to get Dr. Kalinga out of there. My group will go in from the gate side and yours will come in from the west, here. Because we do not know where they are holding him, you will work this bungalow first, it is the home of Snell, the district game warden. Then along the tents and the first three rondavels, stopping in this space if you have not located him."

He looked across at me, and I nodded. My group had been given the easiest assignment, the unguarded side. His would have to comb the customs office, the reception *duka*, the bar-and-dining room shed, and the two rondavels beyond them.

"We meet here, between these rondavels, and take this north path around the rocks which hold the water cistern. Our vehicles will be waiting behind the baobab trees. The ground beyond is marshy but level, and we can get across it to the main road. We will all have knives and carbines, but there will be no shooting except as a last resort. And now let's get blacked up, so that our African friends will not know we are white."

The other men took the dark greasepaint tubes he passed out and went behind the bar. Switching on the lights there and expertly applying the dark makeup, squinting at themselves in the huge mirror.

Holding the tube of greasepaint Trenkel had tossed me, I asked if he knew where General Pangolin's Command Post was, inside the compound. He shook his head.

"No, but it has to be inside the reception *duka* or the dining room."

"And even if we can get Kalinga out, and ourselves, what then?"

"The rest of the armored column will be waiting to join us; we will move on toward the border, five miles this side of Lake Victoria, and invest Sokoto by noon or late afternoon," said Trenkel curtly. It sounded harebrained to me. I don't mind a little action, but like most gamblers I like the edge.

"There are scores of thousands of wild animals grazing around that compound, perhaps as many as two-hundred thousands of them. You can operate an armored column through them, in and out the other side?"

"*Señorito,*" said the gaunt old mercenary, "I am in charge here. You told my employer tonight that I had lost all my wars, and that is true. But I win battles still. If you have courage for it, come with us and I will show you how to win this one. We will get Dr. Kalinga out and immobilize Pangolin's troops."

The Spanish address form he had used was a calculated insult. Staring into his bloodshot eyes, I knew that he had a fever of some kind, malaria or dengue, and probably a shot liver.

"If you have not the stomach for it, go upstairs to the terrace suite and inform Valeuris. I will get another

Number Two, and you can stay here with your Danakil blackbird, safe as houses." He broke off, coughing, bent double by the effort of it.

"Just trying to establish the odds," I answered. "I'll be ready when you are." Going behind the bar, I began to apply the dark greasepaint. In another twenty minutes we were clumping down the wide stairway of Wolf House and loading into the two lead armored cars.

THE sickled moon was nearly down. Through high, broken clouds it cast fitful radiance across the plains. Serengeti covers six thousand square miles, and includes treeless stretches, riverine bush, scrub, swamps, and salt lakes. As I rode along beside the driver of the second car, I could see the black specks massing ahead, spilling across the road. Both armored cars were running without lights, but the one in front slowed to begin plowing through the hump-shouldered, mallet-headed wildebeest herds.

They went bellowing and lunging aside as we parted them in furrows. I saw no lions or leopard, but at this edge of the westering herds I could smell the shambling hyenas.

It was a great night for predators, human and animal. I watched the fleet gazelles bounding out of our path, zebras bucking among them. After we had rolled slowly along for nine or ten miles, parting the endless herds, the lead car flashed its red rear lights and the stolid Dutch driver of my car, who had not spoken to me, turned off to the left. We found potholes, then rolled over spongy marshland to stop behind the grove of thick-bodied baobab trees with the low, pronged branches.

The other car was to our right, already reversing to park facing back toward the road. We did the same. As I stepped out, my boots sank into the yielding turf and I checked my knife and carbine, motioning for the other four to do the same. Trenkel's men had passed out of sight going west, into shadows, and I led the other four troopers to the south. I unhooked the flashlight from my belt and took the carbine off safety.

As we skirted the baobab grove, I could see the pale scars on their trunks, where elephants had peeled away the bark. The game warden's bungalow was dark; I waved the other four men into the shadows at the end of the tent row beyond, and found the same ancient kind of lock on the front door that had been on the rondavel where we had been imprisoned. The plastic strip clicked it open, and I went through the large front room and turned right down the dark corridor.

Wrong way. One flick of the flashlight beam confirmed it. A serving pantry and locked food-storage room, with a door leading under a covered walkway to the outside kitchen hut. I retraced my steps cautiously and found the bedroom at the far end. As I stood in the doorway, flicking the light beam on again, the sleeping English game warden awoke and lunged for the rifle canted by the bed.

"Don't!" I warned, hitting him in the face with the light beam. "Put it down!"

He did, blinking under tousled hair. His wife came awake, too, and started up, muttering. He swept her back flat with his bare right arm, and I flashed the light across my own face.

"We've come to take a prisoner from General Pangolin," I said. "Stay still, you won't be hurt!"

"You black bastard!" the Englishman shouted, and started at me over the end of the bed. *His wife, you see.* I had forgotten I was wearing the black greasepaint, so I had to club him over the head. He dropped flat, sprawling half over the end of the bed.

I snapped the light off and hurriedly explained to the cowering wife, whose terrified breathing I could hear, that we were a white force come on a political errand, no time to explain. But that if she and her husband would remain quiet, with the lights off, no harm would come to them.

"We will," she breathed, and I turned and went back out of the bungalow the way I had come, locking the door again from the outside. Then I stood on the porch for a few seconds, waiting and listening. No sounds disturbed the silence of the Seronera compound except the muted bawlings of the grazing herds around it, and the gruntings of hunting hyenas.

Crossing the path, I joined the other four and we began a systematic search along the tent line. The tents were all dark, stretched tight by guy ropes, and zipped up. We went along them three in front and two behind, but found nobody inside. The first rondavel had its front door open, and the probing flashlight beam found three drunken Marundian soldiers snoring inside.

I was approaching the second rondavel when a sleepy voice ordered me to halt, and a Marundian sentry stepped out of the shadows at the far side. His rifle was leveled. I said "Fool!" in Swahili, holding my arms up, and he came toward me. But he was drunk too, eying me with piggish suspicion when the two rear-side men converged on him. One pinioned his elbows and the other cut his throat with a smooth drawing motion.

He had been guarding nothing, however; the rondavel was empty, so I knew he must be a perimeter sentry. In the next conical hut, weak lights were on and four officers were lounging inside, playing cards under the thatched roof. The two troopers flanking me came near and waited for the order. Should we bypass the rondavel? That was their question.

I decided we had better not, even though their unsnapped sidearms had been tossed carelessly onto the beds. We had been lucky so far, but if an altercation started further along, or in Trenkel's sector of the compound, we couldn't have them in back of us. So I motioned one of the rear guards forward and whispered to them. We would go in one by one.

They nodded and followed as I went striding briskly into the rondavel, nodding to the card players and smashing the hanging light bulb with the butt of my carbine. My target was the officer on the far side of the table, and I went lunging over it at him. The blade, jammed upward in the heel of my hand, caught him rising, under the rib cage. He groaned. Sprawled across the table, I jerked the knife free and found his carotid artery with it.

There were gruntings and curses all around me, so I tumbled on across the table. The white trooper on my right was having his troubles, grappling wildly, so I clubbed his target down and the trooper dropped on him with the knife flailing. There had been no outcry because our surprise had not allowed time for it. The officer I had killed had pumped considerable blood on me, and it was sticky on my hands and soaking the front of my jacket.

The next rondavel was dark. It was the last of our targets, and we were falling back into the three-before-and-two-behind pattern, to surround it, when there was a sudden burst of firing, very near. I didn't take time to unlock that door, just burst the flimsy lock loose with my shoulder and swept the rondavel interior with my flashlight beam. Nobody home.

Sprinting back outside, I waved all four of the others to the dark space between that rondavel and the next one. I was sweating like a sonofabitch. We waited, listening to the firefight down the dusty road. I deployed the other four to protected positions where they could cover the road with their carbines and we waited.

All the outside, pole-mounted lights in Seronera compound flashed on, and more general firing began from the bar-dining-room shed, the reception *tukul,* and the larger rounded hut which was a nightclub for safari parties in more normal times. Marundian soldiers began to debouch into the roadway, firing into the shadows between the first two rondavels. Muzzle flames answered them from the darkness.

We heard running feet, and I wheeled toward the alley behind the rondavels. Flipping on the flashlight with my left hand and cradling the carbine on my right hip. The runaway figure was Claude Kalinga, shoeless, shirtless, and drunk as usual. He might have run all the way back to Keekorok if I had not hooked him with my right arm.

Behind him, limping toward us backward, came Colonel Trenkel and one of his troopers. Marundian soldiers were pressing after them, firing wildly, and we could hear slugs chinking into the mud walls around us. When I dropped my arm, the men in my group went kneeling, firing methodically at every Marundian pursuer.

When Colonel Trenkel nodded at me, I hooked one arm inside Claude Kalinga's left elbow and dragged him after me down the dark path to the right, around the rocky hill which held the water cistern. Behind me, Trenkel was gauging the pursuit, giving orders in a calm voice. When Kalinga and I had rounded the cistern hill and were hustling across the marshy ground toward the baobab grove, he retreated with us. As we ran, I knew that Trenkel's group had not been so fortunate as ours. He had lost two of his men, and I hoped they were dead. If they were only disabled, General Pangolin would kill them slowly.

I got Kalinga into the seat between the Dutch driver and me, and waited for the signal. When the other car hummed to life and drove out we followed it. We were in four-wheel drive, but even so our wheels once hung up, agonizingly, in the marshy turf. The driver was pushing too hard. But I said nothing, and he lifted his heavy foot. The vehicle lunged free and slithered ahead.

On the main highway, we stopped beside Colonel Trenkel's armored car. To our right, lighted vehicles of the Marundian column were streaming out of the compound. Standing in the road beside me, between our two darkened vehicles, Colonel Trenkel watched them come until another coughing fit doubled him up. They were more than half a mile away, and had to make a right-angled turn before they could reach us.

"Now," said Trenkel, straightening up, and the driver of his car handed him a foot-long Schermulli rocket pistol. He held it up and fired. The thick shell shot upward for nearly a thousand feet, and exploded into a scarlet starburst over Serengeti. Dawn was lightening the sky toward the Kenya side as it erupted.

The bloody sign in the sky triggered explosions all

around the Seronera compound. Some were booming near, and others faint and far away, but they seemed to come from all compass points. The explosions were grenades being thrown at every perimeter of the herds around Seronera, and I realized that the colonel had positioned his other men to stampede the browsing herds into the compound.

Bawling, lunging, and bucking, the huge masses of wild animals were being driven inward. They came boiling past our own cars, hooves slashing, crazed with fear, so that the colonel and I had to leap back into the cars. Wave on wave they came, most of them the ungainly, bearded wildebeest. They banged against our armored cars and erupted like a tidal wave into Seronera.

The column of Marundian cars was stopped dead, engulfed. They could neither go forward nor backward; they were isolated islands with the herds plunging around and past them. And Trenkel's grenade throwers kept tightening their cordon, closing in on all flanks. The antipersonnel grenades kept exploding nearer and nearer, visible flashes now in the lightening dawn. The beasts raced into the compound, fear-crazed, ramming into its buildings, butting wildly into other herds converging from all directions.

Trenkel stood watching from his seat for nearly an hour, until all we could see was a sea of plunging backs milling around. Seronera was not an inhabited place anymore; it was only a shattered corral for scores of thousands of maddened wild animals. Then, and only then, he held the Schermulli pistol out of the car's cab and fired it aloft again.

This time the starburst over the Serengeti was pure white light, fissuring into falling streamers. The cannonading of the grenades stopped abruptly. By this time, the waves of animals pounding around and between our armored cars had lessened. I lighted a twisted cheroot with shaking hands, and glanced at Claude Kalinga.

The usually dapper little black man was wearing only pants, and he was exhausted.

"Claude," I said, "it's good to see you again."

Head back against the seat, he nodded politely. "The question is, however, is there a drink in the house?" he enquired.

WE had succeeded in our main objective, recovering Dr. Kalinga so that he could return to Marundi and consummate the wolfram-concession deal with the western consortium. We had even liberated Dorothy Tyson, the Joplin, Missouri flash. She claimed to have spent the hours after Maryam's and my escape singing ballads to her captors and enthralling them with stories of the Jesus freaks in the United States. Since many Marundians had been mission-educated, this was at least a theoretical possibility; at any rate she seemed in buoyant spirits and externally intact.

Where we had missed was General Pangolin. The reptilian dictator had somehow managed to extricate himself and a sizable portion of his troops through the stampeded herds. Much of his equipment had been pounded into scrap under the plunging hooves, but he had made it back to the Marundian border and that meant Colonel Trenkel's mercenary force would meet resistance at Sokoto. This did not seem to bother Trenkel very much.

Claude Kalinga said that Pangolin had gone berserk with rage after my escape, and that he had only stayed alive by promising him to sign over the sequestered funds in the numbered Lausanne accounts. That he had insisted on several drafts of the paper actually conveying these funds, and that the incorrect numbers listed in the agreement would not have entitled Pangolin to make a phone call in Switzerland.

By ten o'clock that morning, Trenkel had established his own losses, only four dead and seventeen wounded. The wounded had been dispatched back toward the Kenya border in three of the requisitioned armored cars. Then his main column started rolling westward toward Lake Victorria and the Marundian border. Shortly before noon, we halted a few miles from it, behind a screen of acacia trees, and heard another automatic fire fight begin. The answering fire was peremptory and soon ceased, so that we knew the border post had been overwhelmed.

Maryam and I sat in the front seat of a lorry which was to take us north to Kampala, the Ugandan capital, and watched Rolf Trenkel standing beside the lead car in the armored column. He had a transceiver at his ear, listening to a report from his advance guard. Watching his gaunt figure in the bleached khaki safari suit, I reflected that the hatchet-faced soldier of fortune had indeed shown me how to win a battle, even if his wars always failed.

He swung behind the wheel, turned his head briefly to snap off a Wehrmacht-type salute to me, and the lead car started rolling out. Dr. Claude Kalinga, O.B.E., and Dorothy Tyson sat beside him, waving goodbye to Maryam and me. Dorothy had confided to Maryam that Claude had promised to set her up in Sokoto, if the mercenaries could reestablish him in the Marundian capital. With the further promise that if the temper of his constituents would permit it, he would marry her.

I didn't blame her. Her resources were small—considerable guts, and a certain kind of intelligence. It was probably her only chance to be important anywhere, even if Claude forgot the marriage promise and ditched her. Otherwise, her only capacity was for being just another nobody back home in Joplin. After being raped in Addis Ababa, she was riding in triumph between a Commander-in-Chief and a deposed President who was possibly returning to power.

What matter if the fiefdom she was entering was mostly a poor land of sunbaked mud huts? It beat the hell out of whatever they do on a rainy night in Joplin.

Claude Kalinga was another matter. An intelligent black man who had been catapulted to power simply because his tribal ancestry and European education had made him unique. And therefore easily susceptible to megalomania. Venal, too, with his only chance for resumed power depending on a sell-out to commercial interests. A jug-hound of purest ray supreme. Still, considerable humor and personal courage. I liked him, and in my business it was not necessary to approve of him.

The long line of armored cars went winding away and vanished in the grove of fever trees fringing the border.

MARYAM Lalibela and I had six days, and we spent them in a bungalow at the Norfolk Hotel in Nairobi. This place sprawls over a lot of ground, has been jerry-built over many decades, and architecturally seems a bastard, rambling construction. But it has a central compound with huge round cages of exotic birds, and its Delamere Terrace, sparkling with bright copper tables, has a charm which cannot be approximated by the sterile downtown Hilton silo.

The dark Danakil girl and I enjoyed an idyll without any restraints or pressures. There was no dissembling in her; naked she came to me in unashamed pursuit of her own pleasure. Her classic-featured face smiled only rarely when we were out at the Lobster Pot or the Three Bells, but an impish sense of humor was always there. We went to the international casino and she was in rapture at winning less than a hundred dollars at roulette. In the snake park, she spent half an hour staring in silent wonder at the vivid orange South African cobra.

I bought her clothes, and she accepted them gladly, never being coy because she had never owned high-fashion garments. After we had swooped through Nairobi's best shops, we had champagne and a fashion show in the bungalow suite. She selected nothing; when we were shown Paris lingerie, gowns or hats, she tried them on dutifully, but always looked at me before deciding. She was so tall, with such a superb figure, that she made them all look good.

But, strangely enough, the dark daughter of the Afar people had little interest in the wisps of lingerie. She had not worn any at all when she was growing up, and the brassieres were an impediment to her firm breasts. Neither did she like the more feminine of the gowns, with their

141

flounces and furbelows. But when I put her in a dark, tailored, and simply cut suit, with her short curly hair topped by a black karakul shako set at a rakish angle, she twirled with glee before the door-length mirror.

"Oh, I am so *fine!*" she murmured. And in an unusual lapse in her perfect English, "My Godness, I am so *fine!*"

She was just that, so we toasted the outfit in champagne a number of times, and I had difficulty in getting her out of it and back in bed.

The days ran along. We got up early to swim in the pool before anyone else was up, and spent several afternoons sitting in the Thorn Tree terrace of the New Stanley Hotel and sipping *aperitifs*. Laughing at the tidal wave of blatant American tourists, the blunt and brusque Teutons, and the quacking Scandinavians.

One afternoon Paul Snyder, my colleague attached to the Nairobi Embassy, dropped by the bungalow to have several drinks with us and announce that Dr. Claude Kalinga had been returned to power in Marundi. General Pangolin was dead. That news seemed remote and inconsequential, but after he was gone Maryam and I laughed at the thought of Dorothy imperial, in whatever land or bed.

Then the time ran out on us, and we came down to the last night together. We lay on the big bed with hands clasped, moonlight from the windows barring our naked bodies and night chirpings and whirrings coming from the aviaries of tropic birds in the courtyard.

Maryam quietly said that if I left her no point would remain to her life. That she would like to come with me, if only for a week or a month, and that she would accept any rules I made about it. That she had guessed something about my business, and would keep my house well whenever I left it, for whatever period I was gone.

I got up, walked into the front room, and poured myself a drink of Jack Daniel's. The bottle had not been opened before; we had not needed anything so strong. Outside, the moonlight spilling into the courtyard seemed intolerably bright. I had loved another black woman once, Jannina, a fashion model from New York. She had also been tall and imperious, and had died violently because I had involved her in my work. *And I had wanted to marry her, to have children out of her. . . .*

Bleakly, taking another drink of the sour-mash whiskey, I thought of Maryam Lalibela as I had about Jannina, a dusky Ruth lost among the alien corn and the ritualistic racial hatreds of my remote Ozark homestead. It would not work.

Going back into the bedroom, I lay down by Maryam again and took her hand. "No," I said, "it's not possible." I did not add that I had faced the problem the day before, and bought her an air ticket back to Ethiopia.

Her hand tightened on mine, and she said without expression, "Perhaps it will be possible for you to come and find me again."

"Not very probable," I answered.

The next morning we had a late breakfast and she put on her tailored suit and rakish black shako, and I put her on the eleven o'clock plane for Addis Ababa. Two hours later, I boarded the Pan-Am flight for Dakar and New York.

The first-class section was not full. As the plane powered off, I sat relaxed; nothing new. I had been out on another bully-boy errand and was going home. *Home?* As the jet flattened out at cruising altitude, I thought of my remote eyrie in the Ozark hills. That place from which I departed unannounced and to which I returned unheralded, after going through my bag of dirty tricks.

I thought of the lament by an early American Indian chieftain. "There runs not a drop of my blood in the veins of any living creature. . . ." That was true of me, too, but I had lived with it because I do not much admire *Homo sapiens* at close range. I might be required, because of my trade, to use violence on them, but nothing in my contracts said I had to associate with them by choice. So I had not.

Still, I now felt a sense of loss. I would have married Maryam Lalibela, had that been possible, and taken her back to my clapboard castle in the southern United States. Love I did not know, never had, but the proud black Danakil girl was the most exciting sexual machine I had ever encountered. In addition, her sense of clan was fierce and her moral standards high.

If we had married, and I had not come back one day from a trip abroad (as was bound to happen) the Nefertiti from the Eritrean Desert would have had my money. The sum of it was not inconsiderable after so many years of playing smash-and-grab. And before I got scragged I would at least have had a lively bedmate, someone interested when I was overdue. It might even have been fun to watch the beautiful black daughter of the Afar people adjusting to western life.

But there was a fatal hitch. I was allowed to punish myself, but not Maryam. The Lord or The Furies; they set us all up in the middle aisle. The Spanish proverb goes that you can take what you want from life. *Take it, and pay for it.* I had lived in the American South too long to believe that Maryam could survive those cretins, with or without me.

The black girl would be in Addis Ababa now, believing that I had used and dumped her. She would continue to be used; a trained nurse is always useful. And I would run out my days getting more staggy and crochety, caring only about myself.

The stewardess, having a half-filled section in first-class, came back to try to sell me something free. I shook my head, knowing that nothing was free, and went on humming.

" 'Make my bed and light the light, I'll be home late tonight. Blackbird, bye bye. . . .' "